The Rookie Bookie is a total touchdown!

"Wertheim and Moskowitz cleverly introduce elements of probability, economics and business. . . . There is a heart to Mitch's tale, and his desire to protect his family and to forge true friendships will resonate with readers. **The sports fan's alternative to *The Lemonade War*.**"
—*Kirkus Reviews*

"Careful to not glorify gambling, this draws attention to its shadowy underside while doling out lessons in honesty and friendship. Mitch's joking tone and genuine desire to gain friends make him a sympathetic character in spite of his lapse in judgment. **A rare offering for both the sports enthusiast and the kid who is always picked last for the team.**"
—*Booklist*

"This is **a cleverly written story, with an astute take on what makes middleschoolers tick.** Strong supporting characters, and a good balance of tension and humor keep the pages turning. While there is a lot of academic content woven into the story—financial literacy, statistics, logic, even a little Shakespeare—it is not heavy-handed. It's all explained in a simple, engaging way, sure to appeal to readers not totally smitten with sports or math. . . . **A thoughtful and highly entertaining read.**"
—*School Library Journal*

"Wertheim and Moskowitz, the writing team behind *Scorecasting*, create a relatable protagonist in Mitch and a fun venue for readers to learn a bit about business, football, and math. Mitch's struggles with bullying are realistic, as are his relationships with his parents and older brother. . . . **This story hits its mark and should intrigue readers** with information about how number-crunching can make an impact on the gridiron."
—*Publishers Weekly*

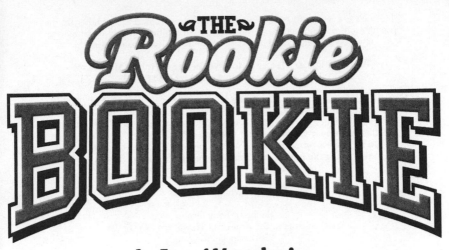

THE Rookie BOOKIE

L. Jon Wertheim
&
Tobias Moskowitz

LITTLE, BROWN AND COMPANY

New York   Boston

Text copyright © 2014 by L. Jon Wertheim and Tobias Moskowitz
Illustrations copyright © 2014 by Neil Swaab

Little, Brown and Company

Hachette Book Group
1290 Avenue of the Americas, New York, NY 10104
Visit us at lb-kids.com

Little, Brown and Company is a division of Hachette Book Group, Inc.
The Little, Brown name and logo are trademarks of Hachette Book Group, Inc.

The publisher is not responsible for websites (or their content) that are not owned by the publisher.

First Paperback Edition: November 2015
First published in hardcover in October 2014 by Little, Brown and Company

Library of Congress Cataloging-in-Publication Data

Wertheim, L. Jon
    The rookie bookie : a novel / L. Jon Wertheim and Tobias Moskowitz ; [illustrator, Neil Swaab].—First edition.
        pages cm
    Summary: "When seventh-grader Mitch Sloan moves to Jonasburg, Indiana, he uses his exceptional skills in math, money, and sports statistics to make friends—but gets in over his head when he starts a football betting ring."—Provided by publisher.
    ISBN 978-0-316-24981-2 (hardcover)—ISBN 978-0-316-24979-9 (paperback) ISBN 978-0-316-24976-8 (ebook)—ISBN 978-0-316-24980-5 (library edition ebook) [1. Football—Fiction. 2. Gambling—Fiction. 3. Middle schools—Fiction. 4. Schools—Fiction. 5. Moving, Household Fiction. 6. Family life—Indiana—Fiction. 7. Indiana—Fiction.] I. Moskowitz, Tobias J. (Tobias Jacob), 1971– II. Swaab, Neil, illustrator. III. Title.
    PZ7.W4783Roo 2014
    [Fic]—dc23

                                                                      2013041705

10 9 8 7 6 5 4 3 2 1

RRD-C

Printed in the United States of America

To Isaac, Josh, Sammy, Sarah, Ben, and Allegra:
Don't start a betting pool at school!

CONTENTS

CHAPTER 1

THE WINNER'S CURSE

Say, "Cheese!"

Jamie Spielberger is a girl, and I do not have a crush on her. Let me repeat that: I. Do. Not. Have. A. Crush. On. Her.

She's just this kid I met when I had my nose buried in the grass in back of the middle school, after I bobbled a pass that would have been a touchdown.

"Wow, that was some catch." A sarcastic voice floated over my head. "You ever consider becoming a professional juggler?"

It was a girl's voice. I rolled over and blinked

up at her. The knees of her jeans were muddy. She was wearing her San Francisco Giants hat backward. She was also grinning and holding my hat.

"Thanks, I'm fine," I said. "No major surgery. Just a few broken bones. I'll walk it off."

"Cool." She handed me my hat and ran off for the next play. "Luke! *Luke!* I'm open, you idiot! Are you blind? If you had one more eye, you'd be a Cyclops!"

Sitting there, I laughed out loud. That was a pretty good line. And she was funny, not mean. She could also catch. When Luke finally saw her and fired off another spiral, just like the one he'd sent at me, the girl nabbed it in midair.

I found out later her name was Jamie.

She was out there most days at lunchtime, when a bunch of guys would show up in the field and start to toss the ball around. Sometimes it was just catching and passing. Some days it would turn into a real game.

I like football, even though I'm not really that good at it. My brother, Kevin, would have caught Luke's pass without blinking. One-handed, probably. But I know how to play, and I'm pretty fast, so I started hanging out around the field at lunchtime. Plus, I was trying to get to know some people. It was my first week as the new kid at Jonasburg Middle School, and I figured if I got to be friends with some of the jocks, it'd be a good start.

The person I really got to know was Jamie.

The next day, she came up to me after the lunchtime game, while we were headed back into school.

"Can I talk to you?" she asked.

Which was weird. Kind of. I mean, she was walking right next to me and talking to me right at that moment, so why did she need to ask me if she *could*? Like it was a big deal?

Wait—*was* it a big deal?

"Sure," I said.

"Alone."

"Um, sure. After fifth period, okay?"

I spent science class wondering what Jamie had to tell me. *Alone.* I just hoped it wasn't a boyfriend-girlfriend, *do you have a crush on me?* kind of thing.

Mrs. Wolff stood in front of the whiteboard talking about tectonic plates and earthquakes and volcanoes—which would usually interest me. But I could barely concentrate; I was distracted wondering what Jamie needed to tell me so badly. I wanted to know, but I didn't want to know.

Maybe it'd be better if we didn't actually have a chance to talk. Maybe she'd forget about whatever it was. When the bell finally rang, I grabbed my folder and bolted out of there, trying to get to my locker before Jamie. I'm Mitch Sloan. She's Jamie Spielberger. We were assigned lockers alphabetically, so hers is right near mine, with only two Smiths and a Spander in between.

I threw my science book on one shelf and got my math book out from another. But I wasn't fast enough. I saw her out of the corner of my eye, taking a small leather notebook out of her bag. She cleared her throat just to be sure I noticed her.

"Oh, hey, Jamie," I said, trying to sound casual. "What did you want to talk to me about before?" I took a deep breath and waited for her answer.

"Trade it," she said, turning the knob on her lock.

"Huh?"

"Trade it."

"Trade what?"

She looked up, frustrated, and put a hand on her hip. "Did you or didn't you get the first pick in the seventh-grade fantasy football draft?"

Whew. None of that awkward girl-boy stuff. It was a total relief. I had to wipe a stupid grin off my face.

"Yeah," I said proudly. "I got the first pick out of the ten teams, and I—"

"Trade it," she said again, cutting me off. "Everyone wants it, and they think it's more valuable than it really is. Sure, you'll get a good player. But then you won't go again until the last pick of the second round."

"So?"

"So you're better off with picks ten and eleven or picks nine and twelve than you are with picks one and twenty."

Wait. Whoa. How did she know that?

The thing is, I knew it, too. I had totally been planning to trade that first pick. Everybody wants it, so they think it's special, worth more than it is.

There's even a name for when something like this happens: the winner's curse. Which means you do whatever you can to get something you really want because you thought everybody else really wanted it, and it turns out it wasn't worth it.

But I was surprised—shocked, really—that Jamie knew about the winner's curse, too. I'd never met any other kids who understood this kind of thing.

And by the time I got my brain unstuck and my mouth working again, Jamie was already walking away down the hall, the leather notebook poking out from her back pocket.

"Thanks, Jamie," I yelled to her down the hall. "I was going to do that, anyway."

Two hours and eight minutes later—not that I was counting—the second bell rang and it was official: I had survived my first week at Jonasburg Middle School. Ever since my first week of kindergarten, I'd always felt pretty good on Friday afternoons. But this day, I was feeling extra pretty good. I'd learned my way around the building. I hadn't gotten into any trouble with my teachers; I even liked some of them. I'd learned the names of a few other sports freaks and gotten invited to join their fantasy football league. Plus, I'd gotten the first pick in the draft.

And there was Jamie. She seemed kind of cool, and it looked like she might be interested in some of the same stuff I was, like anything having to do with football.

I like all sports, really. Football, baseball, basketball, you name it. Actually, I like talking and thinking about sports more than I like playing them. Probably because I'm much better at it. I like figuring out strategy and how to win. That's why I love fantasy sports—no dropped passes, just who to pick and who to play. But there's one other thing I like almost as much, maybe even more, and I might as well tell you up front.

I love money and business.

Okay, before you decide that this makes me a greedy kid who doesn't care about the things that really matter, let me explain.

See, most kids in my grade want to be famous

athletes or singers or actresses. That would be cool, but if you got picked last for teams as often as I have, eventually you'd give up the dream of becoming the next Derek Jeter or LeBron James. Besides, even if I could play, I'd rather *own* the Yankees or the Heat than *play* for the Yankees or the Heat.

Instead of being a sports hero, I want to be the next Warren Buffett.

The other day I wrote that in one of those first-week-of-school autobiography assignments. Kevin read it and got all confused. "Buffett? Is he, like, the guy that invented all-you-can-eat?"

"No. That's pronounced buff-fay," I told him. "This is Buff-ett. He's an investor. A financier. Probably the most successful investor of all time."

"Oh yeah?" he said, barely looking up.

"He's like a gardener, but he tries to grow money instead of flowers and plants. And he's worth more than fifty billion dollars."

"Right," said Kevin. "Because money's the most important thing in the world."

"Look at it this way," I said, trying to put it in terms Kevin would care about. "He could buy every team in Major League Baseball and the National Football League at once. He could give every single American a hundred dollars, and he'd *still* be a billionaire. He could—"

"Okay," Kevin barked. "He's rich. I get it."

But as usual, Kevin didn't get it. "I *don't* care about being rich," I told him. "I just want to make a lot of money."

"That doesn't make any sense," he said, looking back at the TV.

"Okay," I said, sighing. "You know how when you go to the arcade, you get as many tickets as you can playing Skee-Ball and Pop-A-Shot and Whac-A-Mole and all that? You do everything you can to win. You combine tickets with your friends. You hustle like crazy. After all that, you get to the window and you trade your tickets in for some stupid keychain or some inflatable pillow you never use."

"I guess," said Kevin.

"Well, that's how I feel about money. It's not just about the stuff you can buy. It's about finding new ways to make it. Trading. Avoiding traps. It's the game of it."

Kevin looked up and studied me. "Don't you want money to get a really cool car like a Ferrari Testarossa or an electric guitar or some new clothes?" You see, Kevin's sixteen, a junior in high school, about to get his driver's license, and crazy about cars and clothes and all that junk.

"Nah, those are just things," I told him. "I don't need *things*." (Though owning a sports team one day would be supercool.) "Money can help you *do* stuff that no one else can," I continued. "Think of it as something you can trade with anyone for almost anything. Or you can help people who need it. Did you know Warren Buffett is giving away most of his fortune—"

"Wait," Kevin cut me off. "You mean you want to make money just so you can give it away? That's the stupidest thing I've ever heard. You're so weird." He snorted and walked out of the room laughing.

───

The problem is that some of the other kids in seventh grade think my hobby is weird, too. Check that. *Most* of them think it's weird. Same with their parents. And same with *my* parents.

Mom and Dad are both artists. My mom mostly paints, and my dad is a potter. When we lived in California, they rented a small gallery where they sold their art. But both of them admit that they don't have what they call "a head for business." Actually, they brag about it. When I get going, talking about business stuff, they get impatient.

"Mitch, money's not everything," my mom says a lot. "All that talk about profit and loss, savings this, spending that. It gets—"

Kevin cut her off this time. "It gets *annoying.* Admit it, Mom."

My mom paused, clearly struggling to say the right thing. "I wasn't going to put it quite like that," she said slowly. "But let's just say I do wish you talked about money a little less sometimes, Mitch."

Annoying.

I get that a lot. Between Kevin and kids at school, I've been called that since I was born. It's one of those words people always seem to use for short people like me. Tall people might be doofy or goofy or gawky or awkward. But how often are tall people described as "annoying"? Not very.

I used to be okay with the word "annoying" because I told myself it meant that I was smarter than the person calling me that, and that made them uncomfortable. But right before we left California, I was watching a business show on television and heard the head of a big company tell the host that one of the most important skills in business is to be able to make everyone around you feel comfortable. "You don't want to do business with someone who *annoys* you and gets under your skin," the man said. "You just don't."

Ever since, I'd been trying really hard not to annoy anybody. But sometimes it just seemed to happen.

Like Saturday morning. I woke up late and ate a bowl of Cap'n Crunch, the all-time best cereal in the history of the world, and then I rode over to my parents' shop. The store is barely a mile from our house, and I learned a shortcut that would get me there on my bike in less than eight minutes.

When I walked in, there were no customers.

Dad was sitting on a stool behind the counter, playing his guitar, not seeming to mind that he wasn't selling paintings or making any money. It was like the California gallery all over again.

"What's up?" I asked.

"Just chillin'," he said, moving the fret bar on his guitar. "Chillin' like Bob Dylan."

"Nobody says that anymore, Dad."

"Maybe not now. But it'll come back. Cool things always come back in fashion. And then you can tell your friends that I was ahead of the curve."

"Slow Saturday?" I asked, looking around the empty store.

"Understatement of the day," said my dad. "Two people came and looked at these flowerpots but decided that fifty dollars was too much money to pay."

"Too much money compared to what?" I asked.

"Not compared to anything," he said, starting to pluck his guitar strings. "Just too expensive for flowerpots, I guess."

"Maybe that's the problem," I said. "How about giving your customers a comparison so they think fifty dollars is a good price for those flowerpots?"

"Sorry, Mitch," my dad said, still not looking at me, "I don't follow."

I paused. Sometimes—okay, lots of times—people don't react so well when I try to explain stuff like this. I know it's one of the things that makes me *annoying*, but the thing is, sometimes I have good ideas. And my parents really needed to make this store work.

"People like to compare stuff," I told Dad. "Is fifty dollars a lot of money? Depends what for, right? It's cheap if you're buying, like, a plane ticket to Europe. It's expensive if you're buying something like a candy bar."

"Art isn't a candy bar, Mitch," my dad said a little too patiently. "Each piece is unique. It's not like there's a rack of my pots down at the gas station."

"Yeah, I know," I agreed. "You have your own shop, so you can create the comparisons yourself. Even better."

"I still don't follow," said Dad.

"Okay," I responded. "How about making a flowerpot that's bigger? Same design. Same color. Same shape. But just a little bigger. Charge, say, a hundred dollars for it. Suddenly the fifty-dollar pot will actually seem like a bargain."

Dad paused. "Maybe," he eventually mumbled to himself, and then started to play a few chords again.

I sighed. It was a good idea. But the minute I tried talking to my dad about money, he only listened for about thirty seconds before tuning me out.

And you know what—*that* was annoying. Considering the reason why we really left California.

CHAPTER 2

TWO FOR THE PRICE OF ONE

Trying to give my dad advice made me think about Jamie trying to tell me what my fantasy football first draft pick was really worth. So I asked my dad if I could borrow his computer and looked up her address. There was only one Spielberger in town, so I got my bike and headed over.

I didn't call ahead. That would feel kind of, I don't know, like a date. And this wasn't a date, because I. Do. Not. Have. A. Crush. On. Jamie. Spielberger. (Remember?)

I just thought that maybe—*maybe*—she wouldn't tune me out like the rest of the world did when I started talking. We had a lot in common. It was worth a shot.

When I got there, I rang the doorbell, and her mom opened the door. Boy, her mom. My mom was at home in her ripped-up jeans and her old college sweatshirt, splattered all over with paint. Jamie's mom was dressed like she was going to work out—yoga pants, tight top, running shoes—but she had makeup on and her hair was shiny and all her fingernails were glowing this peachy-pink color. She just wasn't what I'd pictured for Jamie's mom at all. But she did seem really happy to see me.

"Jamie!" she called, beaming this big happy smile. "You have a visitor!"

When Jamie came downstairs, she looked just like she did at school—baggy T-shirt, jeans with a hole in one knee, baseball cap.

"Oh, honey," her mom said. "I know I washed those other jeans for you, and there's a skirt—"

"This is *fine*, Mom." Jamie looked at me like she didn't know who I was for a second, and I felt like maybe showing up without calling had been a bad idea.

Then Jamie grinned, and her mom sighed and went away.

"Hey, Mitch. What's up?"

"Hey, Jamie. I just thought maybe...you want to look over the fantasy football picks?" I waved a printout at her, and she shrugged.

"Sure."

I'd put in **boldface** the names of players I wanted to pick. She made a scowling face as she looked at my list. "Classic mistake," she said. "You don't have enough guys from lousy teams. You're drafting players, not picking who you think is going to win the Super Bowl."

She had a point.

And after we'd done some football talk, it seemed kind of natural to go out into the backyard and start throwing a ball back and forth. Her dog, Pepper, a big golden retriever, came out, too, and ran back and forth between us, following the football each time we threw.

"So," Jamie said, zinging a pass into my hands. "Question: What are you doing here?"

"Throwing a football?" I guessed.

"I mean here in Indiana, dummy. Why'd your family move?"

Oh. Right. Just what I wanted to talk about. "A bunch of reasons," I said. "My mom grew up around here. My dad kept complaining that there were too many other artists trying to sell their stuff in San Francisco. Too much competition, you know? And stuff. So we moved. Might as well live where the houses are cheaper and you don't have to pay tons of money in tolls every time you need to cross a stupid bridge."

She nodded like that wasn't the lamest explanation she'd ever heard, and I was hoping the subject would die. "So whattaya think? How do you like it here?"

"Well," I said, stalling, "the kids here are basically the same as they were at home. Some are taller and some are shorter. Some are shy and some talk a lot."

"It has to be *a little* different here," she said skeptically.

"Sure. Nobody talks about surfing and no one rides a skateboard to school. They're more into sports here, which is fine by me. And before, the middle school wasn't attached to the high school, so I didn't go to school in the same building as my brother. Now I do."

"So is that good different or bad different?"

"Neither, really. Just different."

"It's kind of cool that you have a brother." She threw the football a little harder. "I sometimes wish there were other kids around here. To take some of my parents' attention off me, you know?"

"Yeah." I sent her back a pretty good spiral. "But I have to say the kids are nicer here. And smarter, too."

Jamie whooped. "If you think we're smarter, you haven't been here long," she said. "Trust me, some of the kids here are not the sharpest Crayolas in the box."

"Huh?" I said.

"There are kids here so dumb they would wait for a stop sign to turn green. They would bring a big spoon to a Super Bowl party. They would—"

"I get it," I said, cutting her off. "But you know what? None of the kids at Jonasburg have stuffed my head into a toilet. So, overall, I like it."

She stopped throwing the ball and stared at me.

"That happened to you?"

"Back in California, yeah," I said. "Hey, let me ask *you* a question. What's with the notebook you're always carrying around?"

"I have four words for you, not necessarily in the right order: Your. Business. None. Of."

She said it with a smile, though.

———

It didn't take long before I figured out what Jamie was talking about when she said "not the sharpest Crayolas in the box." During Mrs. Henry's class the next week, I tried to jump into a conversation with two kids at my table. Clint Grayson, a big eighth grader whose muscular arms popped out of the overalls he was wearing and whose breath smelled like Cool Ranch Doritos, was telling everyone about an R-rated movie his uncle let him see.

"It was so awesome," he said. "People were crushed under a gigantic tidal wave and there was a huge flood, so they had to evaporate the whole city!"

I started laughing. No one else did. Clint fixed his gaze on me.

Before I could say *evacuate, not evaporate*, I stopped myself. The new kid telling an eighth grader how to talk? Not the way to make friends.

Maybe the way to make myself kind of *annoying*.

And it turned out to be a good thing I didn't correct Clint Grayson's vocabulary. Because when I showed up for football practice, there he was.

Like I said, I like watching football more than I like playing football. That's how it is with me and most sports. But I thought I'd try out for the football team after watching Kevin.

Before we moved to Jonasburg, Kevin had never played on a football team in his life. He showed up for practice in August before high school had even started. By the end of the week, he was the starting wide receiver on the team, and an assistant coach told him that if he kept improving, he could be in line for a college scholarship.

Of course, this got him instant friends. Instant respect. Instant cred with any girl he wanted to ask out. Sports make Kevin's life so much easier. So I figured I would at least go through tryouts for the Jonasburg Middle School team. Maybe the kids here wouldn't be faster and stronger and just plain better than me, the way they always were in California. That was my thinking, anyway. My wishful thinking.

Because when I got to the field after school, I instantly saw that it wasn't going to be like throwing the ball around a little after lunch. The other kids were older. And tons bigger.

And there was Clint Grayson, the eighth grader. He *looked* like a football player. He brought his own helmet and came with eye black already streaked on his upper cheeks. When I walked by him and nodded, he either didn't recognize me or just pretended not to. Instead, he spit on the grass and kept walking.

The coach, Mr. Bob Williams, was also the coach of the high school team. The schools used to have different coaches, but to save money, the town put Coach Williams in charge of both teams last year. He wore a whistle around his neck and these shiny shorts that looked like they were made from the same material as my mom's swimsuit. He had a T-shirt that was two colors: gray where he wasn't sweaty and black where he was soaked through.

Kevin had told us that Coach Williams had been a great high school player for Jonasburg before he hurt his knee or something. I searched "Bob Williams" online and, sure enough, he was a star who "led his team to the Indiana state championship" and was "heavily recruited." Then, during college, he "suffered a torn ACL", which I think is something in your knee. I've heard of pro players tearing this and they are usually out for the season and sometimes their careers. As far as I could tell, he never played football again.

He was older now, but Coach Williams still looked like a real athlete. He had broad bulges for muscles, almost like a suit of armor, and cables of veins covered his arms. Walking around the field, he looked at home, the way Kevin does. You know those adults you want to impress? He was one of them.

At the start of practice, he brought us to midfield and had us circle around him. "Boys, take a knee," he said slowly as we shifted into position. "Glad you had the courage to come today. This season, we're gonna play hard. We're gonna play as a team. But most of all, we're gonna play brave. And just by being here you're showing you're brave."

We passed around a clipboard and wrote our names and our grades. Then he read the names. "Herman. Smith. Jeffrey. Kumar..." Hands went up.

"Grayson." Clint's hand shot up.

"Excellent," said Coach Williams. "I heard you can kick the ball a mile."

"Yessir," said Clint.

Finally, he got to me. "Sloan."

My hand shot up like I had a jet pack on my elbow.

"Wait a second," said Coach Williams. "You're Kevin Sloan's brother?"

I nodded.

He grinned.

"Think we might have ourselves a ringer," he said to no one in particular.

Luckily we weren't practicing in helmets and pads and no one was getting tackled today. Because otherwise I might have gone right from the football field of Jonasburg Regional High School to the emergency room of Jonasburg Regional Hospital. The other kids weren't just bigger. They were faster and stronger and way more coordinated.

We had a footrace. I came in last out of forty-five. We had a contest to see who could do the most push-ups in sixty seconds. I was last out of forty-five again. Clint Grayson came in first both times. And Coach Williams was right. He *could* kick the ball a mile.

For one drill, Coach Williams threw us passes, zinging the ball at what seemed like a hundred miles an hour. I didn't catch a pass, not one single time. "Gotta hustle, little Sloan dude," Coach Williams barked at me. I didn't know what was worse: that he was scolding me, that he didn't know my name was Mitch, or that he was already calling me "little."

For the last half hour, we split into four teams to play two scrimmages of flag football. There were eleven kids on each team. With forty-five kids, that left an odd man out. Or an odd kid out.

Me.

"Stand by my side," Coach Williams told me. "Help me observe, little man."

I stood next to him, watching. On one play that started at midfield, a quarterback—a kid with long hair I recognized from Lunch A—ran backward, then to his right, then backward some more. Just as he was about to be caught, he dumped a short pass to a teammate. As soon as the receiver caught the pass, he was slapped on the back and pushed almost to the goal line.

Coach Williams made a face that looked like he had just smelled a dirty diaper. Or Clint Grayson's Dorito breath. He blew his whistle and walked onto the field. "What happened there, fellas?"

No one answered. So he turned to me. "Little man," he said, his voice piercing the air, "what happened?"

I wasn't sure what to say. So I paused and then blurted out the first thing that popped into my head. "The receiver should have dropped the pass."

"Unlike you, some of us actually try to catch the ball," said Clint. The other players started to laugh.

But Coach Williams spun around and looked at them. "Exactly!" he said. "The receiver should have dropped the ball." The laughter stopped. "Tell us why, Little Sloan."

Now I had a little more confidence. "Because everyone was so far behind the line of scrimmage and the defense was so nearby, it made no sense to catch the pass. Drop it and it's incomplete and you're back on the thirty-yard line. Catch it and you need to run halfway to Illinois just to get back to the line of scrimmage."

Again, there were some chuckles led by Clint Grayson. By now I had become a pro at distinguishing laughs. These weren't the *Hey, Mitch is a smart guy!* laughs. They were the *Mitch is annoying* laughs.

I just didn't get it. I was right. I knew I was right. What's so annoying about that?

But thankfully, Coach Williams had my back. "Exactly! Right on, Little Sloan! There's no reason to catch that pass! It sounds funny, but you're better off taking the incompletion. Gotta use your heads, guys!"

A few minutes later, Gene Beech—a skinny seventh grader who played trumpet with me in band class—had to leave practice to get to a Boy Scout meeting. Coach Williams turned to me. "Get in there, Little Sloan," he said. "Let's see you put your football smarts to some good use!"

Yeah, that wasn't going to happen. Clint Grayson was playing quarterback. He dropped back and, after realizing that no one else was open, threw me a pass. It was like my hands were made of cement. *Doink.* The ball brushed against my fingertips and slid away, falling to the ground.

"Come on!" yelled Clint, stomping his foot. "You gotta catch that, kid!"

I hoped Coach Williams hadn't been looking, but then I heard his booming voice. "Sloan!" he yelled. "Catch the ball with your hands, not just your eyes!"

Defense was even worse. On the very first play, I was supposed to cover David Chu, one of the few Asian kids at Jonasburg Middle School. I lined up next to him, and when the center hiked the ball to the quarterback, David jogged about five yards and I stayed with him every step. *Whew*, I thought, *finally someone I can keep up with.*

That thought was still swirling in my brain when David suddenly sped up and sprinted down the field. If you had been watching, you might have thought that he was running with a tailwind and I was running against a headwind. I turned back in time to see the ball make a perfect arc over my head and land in David's hands.

With everyone else on the field yelling, I took off after David. But he was gone. Around the time he crossed the goal line, I started to stumble. I don't know if I tripped over a patch of crabgrass or my shoelaces, or if I was just being clumsy. But I broke my fall with my wrists and my knees. Even the landing was awkward. Lying there on the ground, I practically could hear Jamie's smack talk. *You're so slow, you'd come in third in a two-man race. You could lose a race against a parked car. You're so short, you could play handball against a curb....*

I looked over and saw Coach Williams on the sidelines wearing a slight smile. I could read his mind, too. *Guess the big brother got all the athletic genes.*

I stood up, covered in dirt and grass, and heard Clint's voice. "Now you look like crap *and* play like it." He snickered and spit on the grass.

Luckily, a few minutes later, practice was over. Dad picked me up. He could probably tell I was bummed, because he kept cracking these corny jokes on the way home.

"Let me guess: You wanted to play quarterback because you thought it was a refund."

"Very funny," I grumbled.

"Hey, maybe this'll cheer you up," he said. "I tried your idea yesterday. A man bought three of those flowerpots I had in the back of the store. I put a price of fifty dollars on one, and a price of a hundred dollars on another that was only slightly bigger. I overheard the guy whispering to his wife, 'Wow, Denise, it's like getting two for the price of one!'"

Okay, so on the one hand, it looked like I wasn't going to play football at Jonasburg Middle School *and* I'd just looked like an idiot in front of forty-four kids I was trying to impress *and* the coach had kept calling me "little"...but on the other hand, I'd helped my dad make some money.

Maybe the day wasn't a total loss.

CHAPTER 3

LIARS CAN FIGURE AND FIGURES CAN LIE

After a couple of weeks, Kevin was catching rides to and from school with his new teammates and friends. It sometimes seemed like he was born with...well, you know those instruction manuals that come with DVD players or video games? You never read them, but you keep them anyway? It seemed like Kevin was born with one of those instruction manuals for life. Sports, girls, video games...everything (except school) always came easy to him. As if he just knew what to do.

Since Kevin had all his new friends to ride with, on the days that Mom and Dad drove me to school, I had them to myself. Which was kind of nice—I'll admit it—but also had its downside. Sometimes I felt like a witness in one of those courtroom TV shows, getting attacked by lawyers asking a million questions. On Monday, they attacked from both sides.

"What are you going to do in school today?" Mom asked.

"I dunno," I said.

"What subjects are you digging?" my dad asked, trying to sound cool.

Mom jumped in. "Are the other kids nice? Do you want to invite someone over?"

"Mitch," my dad said, raising his eyebrows at me in the rearview mirror. "How's the seventh-grade talent?"

I could barely get a word in if I wanted to, so I looked out the window and pretended I wasn't listening. I was hoping they would lose interest if I ignored them.

"Mitch? Talent? Are there any foxes?"

"Foxes?"

"Girls, Mitch," my father said. "Any cute girls?"

Is there anything more annoying than parents trying to find out if you have a girlfriend? Oh, wait. I forgot. There is. A parent who tries to find out if you have a girlfriend and uses a lame-o, old-fashioned word like "foxes."

The truth is that, while she wasn't my *girlfriend* (Remember? I. Do. Not. Have. A. Crush. On. Her.), Jamie was becoming my best friend. She was in three of my classes, and even though I would never sit at her table at lunch, sometimes we sat next to each other on the bus ride home.

She was so not like the other girls. She wasn't picky about food, she didn't get grossed out by blood or mud or guys spitting loogeys, and she sure didn't seem to care about clothes or shoes or who had a crush on who. She only had strong opinions— the strongest opinions—when it came to sports.

"You actually *like* Johnson?!" she said to me after school on the bus. "You're joking, right? He stinks worse than Clint Grayson's laundry basket! You'd be better off with *Mr.* Johnson." Mr. Johnson was the music teacher, and his thick glasses and wooden cane made him look like he was about ninety years old.

"What?" I said, feeling like I had to defend myself. "He's good. He ran for nearly a thousand yards last season."

"Yeah, against lousy teams and when the game was out of reach," she said. "Liars can figure and figures can lie."

"What's that mean?" I said.

"You know those statistics that announcers are always mentioning?" she said in the same tone of voice I use when I explain things to Kevin.

"Sure."

"Well, sometimes those numbers are helpful. Other times they don't say much at all. Like, you know how announcers talk about a team, and say, 'They've won three of their last four games!'"

"Yeah."

"You know that means they've only won three of their last five games."

"How do you know that?"

"Because if the team had won more than that,

the announcers would have told you," she said. "Think about it. If they had won four games out of their last five, that would've sounded even more impressive. But they clearly didn't. That's why the announcer said three out of four. A team wins three of the last four games and you think, *Oh, they're doing really well.* But a team wins three of the last five games and you think, *So what? That's barely half.*"

I had never thought of it that way. As usual, she was right. I tried to change the subject so I wouldn't have to admit it. "What's your least favorite sport?" I asked her.

"I would say golf," she responded. "But anything you do while wearing checkered pants and a belt can't even be considered a sport. And have you seen some of these golfers? They're so fat, they sweat gravy. They're not athletes!"

O-kay. Changing the topic to football, I asked her: "You think Baltimore has a chance to beat Pittsburgh on Sunday?"

"Yeah," she shot back.

"Think they'll win by more than four points?"

"Yup."

"Wanna put your money where your mouth is?"

"How much?" she said suspiciously. But I could tell that she was considering it.

"Let's say five bucks."

"That's half my weekly allowance!" she said. "But..." She hesitated. "Okay, sure."

I put out my hand to shake.

"Wait," she said.

"What?"

"Isn't betting, like, illegal?" Jamie asked, sounding uncertain.

"You said your uncle Gary likes to bet on NFL games every Sunday."

"Yeah, but Uncle Gary lives in Las Vegas."

"Jamie," I said, "who's going to find out?"

"Maybe it's against school rules," she said haltingly.

"I don't remember hearing anything about that," I said. "And we're not in school; we're on the bus. Besides, *when* you lose, you can pay me outside of school if it makes you feel better," I added with a grin.

Jamie narrowed her eyes and looked at me, and then smiled. "Baltimore to win by more than four points? Deal."

We shook on it. (But not before she pretended to spit on her hand before shaking.) As our palms brushed together, I couldn't help noticing that her hands were bigger, dirtier, and rougher than mine. I also couldn't help noticing that she was carrying her leather notebook again.

"What's in that thing, anyway?" I asked.

She sighed. "Promise not to tell anyone?"

"Promise."

"You know how some people love to play violin or run or draw?"

"Sure," I said, thinking to myself, *Or love to make money.*

"Well, I love to write," she said. "It doesn't seem like work, the way math or science does. Ideas and different ways to describe things come into my head, like, sort of naturally. So I try to write them down. It's hard to explain."

"Cool," I said. "You should try to write a book one day."

"Maybe I will," she said.

———

That Friday at school, we had something called a "pep rally." I'd never seen anything like it. It was crazy. But it seemed totally normal for everyone else. The Jonasburg Regional High School football team was opening its season that night, and it was all anyone could talk about. A lot of store windows had "Go Jo" signs in them.

I knew that Indiana was a big basketball state. Before we moved, Kevin and I saw the movie *Hoosiers* and watched basketball games of Indiana University (who my Mom grew up rooting for). We made Mom and Dad promise to take us to an Indiana basketball game, hopefully against Purdue—their rivals. Kevin already hated Purdue, and Mom and Dad had even been known to make a gently sarcastic comment about them (that was about as mean as they ever actually got).

But the people here clearly liked their football, too. As we entered the gym for the pep rally,

I realized I was the only person not wearing the school's maroon and gold colors.

"Where's your school spirit?" Clint Grayson barked as he bumped my shoulder, sneering and looking genuinely upset. "This ain't wherever the heck you came from, you know."

"No one told me—" I started to say, but Clint cut me off.

"Do you know what we do around here with traitors?" he asked, laughing and looking at the kids next to him. Then he punched his left fist into his right palm, making a noise that sounded like an egg being cracked. Clint's buddies laughed, and they all pushed past me.

When everyone settled into their seats on the bleachers, Mr. Pearlman, the principal of the high school and the middle school, stood up. He looked like a duck as he walked in a waddling kind of way to the microphone.

Mr. Pearlman looked even more nervous than usual. All the middle school and high school was there, and pretty much all their parents, too. And even though I was the new kid in town, I already knew that nobody really liked Mr. Pearlman, not even the teachers. Behind me, I overheard Mrs. Liu, the health teacher, whispering to one of the other teachers that he was a "bad communicator" and was "going to chase the good teachers off."

As Mr. Pearlman spoke in a serious voice, the speakers crackled and the sound echoed off the walls. He talked about "our proud tradition" and "our expectation of excellence." It took me a second to realize that he wasn't talking about the school itself—kids getting top grades or teachers doing a good job in the classroom or the library having enough books. He was talking about the football team. Boy, they take their sports seriously around here. And I could see what Mrs. Liu was talking about. He wasn't very inspiring.

As he went on about "a return to glory" and how "we all hope for a show of dramatic improvement," I remembered what Jamie had said on the bus, about what sports announcers say and what they really mean.

What Mr. Pearlman really meant was: *The team stunk last year, and if we don't get better, it will mean trouble.*

Coach Williams was next to speak, and he seemed a little nervous at first, nodding over at Mr. Pearlman. But then he started talking about the team and the season, and it was like a general from one of those army movies, talking passionately to the soldiers. "I can only put eleven guys on the field at once!" he said. "But there's no limit to how many of you can support us from the bleachers! I want *you* to be our twelfth man!" I found myself nodding in agreement. Then, as I looked around, I saw that everyone else was nodding, too.

Next, Coach Williams turned to his players. "I can't promise we'll win every game, but I can promise you this, guys," he said, his face now turning red. "I'm gonna give you everything I got as a coach."

"Everything I got"? He meant "everything I have." But I kept that to myself. The anti-annoyance pledge and all.

"In exchange, I need you to give me everything

you got as players. I'm gonna give one hundred and ten percent to make you better players. But you have to give each other one hundred and ten percent, too!"

I wondered how anyone could give more than 100 percent. It's not like there's extra credit. I mean, 100 percent is the most you can possibly give, right? I kept this thought to myself, too.

Coach Williams wasn't through. "Iron sharpens iron! And you are going to sharpen each other!"

Everyone cheered like crazy.

Coach Williams then announced the players, and they stood one by one. Meanwhile the cheerleaders did these weird kicks. When Coach Williams got to Kevin, he called him a "California import." I thought that made him sound like an avocado or something. But it still must have felt good to Kevin to get noticed like that. He stood up from his folding chair and raised his hand.

"K-Dog!" someone yelled.

How had he already gotten a nickname? Typical. People were still learning my real name.

When Coach Williams was done, the band

played the Jonasburg fight song. Everyone stood and the mood turned serious. I had no idea what the words were, so I faked it, trying to fit in. (If you mouth the word "watermelon" over and over, you can pretty much look like you know the words to any song.) But Clint, just a few seats down from me, saw what I was doing.

"Remember what I said about traitors," he hissed.

CHAPTER 4

IT PAYS TO KNOW THE SCORE

That night, Mom, Dad, and I piled into the car and went to Kevin's first game as an Indiana football player. Actually, it was his first game as a football player, period. But that didn't stop him from being totally psyched, like he'd been living here all his life.

The Jonasburg Whales opened the season against the Ikeville Eels. I wondered why two schools in the guts of America, hundreds of miles from an ocean, had sea creatures for mascots. Once again,

I shared this thought with the only person who wouldn't find it annoying—me.

I walked into the stadium with my parents but hoped I wouldn't have to sit with them. It wasn't that they embarrassed me, but . . . well, okay, maybe they embarrassed me a little. Mom had come right from the studio and was wearing a denim jacket spattered with paint, and her head was wrapped in a rainbow-colored bandanna. Dad had on his leather jacket with tassels and a beret. Let's just say they stood out from the other parents.

We were passing the concession stand when I saw Ben Barnes, Avni Garg, and Jacob Alexander, all from my grade and all in the fantasy football league. "Hey, Mitch!!" one of them yelled.

Okay, maybe it wasn't exactly a yell. I may have imagined those exclamation points. But that's how it sounded to my ears. And it felt pretty good.

I turned to my parents. Dad was already waving me off. "Go with your friends," he said. "But unless you want to walk home, find us after the game."

"Got it."

As I left to sit with Ben, Avni, and Jacob, I could see Mom smiling. And I knew why.

All summer I'd heard (and overheard) my parents whispering about "Mitch's adjustment." Kevin would be fine. It was me they were worried about. I got good grades, sure, but I couldn't play sports. I annoyed people. I didn't usually fit in.

And now here I was, at my first football game, and people were yelling (or at least calling) my name. Mom figured I was making friends already. No drama, no problems. Take *that*, adjustment period!

The mood turned sour, though, once the game started. Kevin caught three passes, which might sound like a lot, but they were the only three passes that Jonasburg completed. The quarterback, Neil Butwipe (I'm not making it up, that was really his name, though he claimed it was pronounced *boot-wee-pay*), was...let's just say not that great. Over and over again, he would throw incomplete passes and the crowd would groan. (And can you imagine having "Butwipe" stitched in shining gold on the back of your jersey for every game?)

"Aim the dang ball! Either that or move over

and let someone else play quarterback!" yelled one woman—the backup quarterback's mom, I bet.

"Who'd he throw that to?" one man wearing a Jonasburg jacket yelled in frustration. "I have a vacuum cleaner that doesn't suck this much."

Not bad trash talk. Jamie would be impressed. But even so, it wasn't really nice or fair.

In the first place, Neil was a kid, not a pro. Plus, it wasn't all his fault. In history class we learned about non-aggression treaties, when one country agrees not to fight another. Jonasburg's offensive line played like they had signed a non-aggression treaty with the other team. *What's that? You want to sack our quarterback? Why, go right ahead! Right this way!* If there had been a stat for the number of grass stains on your uniform, Neil would have gotten game MVP honors.

But the offensive line was only part of the issue. The real problem was something that the fans in the bleachers didn't yell about, like they didn't even notice it. But I did.

Coach W. was making bad decisions. I mean, *awful* decisions.

He was good at teaching players *how* to do things, whether it was throwing passes into the wind or tucking the ball into your body when you ran so the defense couldn't strip it away. And he was a master motivator; I'd seen that at the pep rally. Kevin announced after his first practice that he would "run through a brick wall for that guy."

But the choices Coach Williams made out there on the field sometimes didn't make sense. In the second quarter, Ikeville was leading 13–0. Jonasburg scored its first touchdown when Neil scrambled, couldn't find an open receiver, and ran the ball into the end zone to make it 13–6. Instead of kicking an extra point, Coach Williams had the Whales try a two-point conversion, which didn't make any sense. Even if the two-pointer had been successful, Jonasburg would be down by five and still need a touchdown to move ahead. Making a two-point conversion is a lot harder than kicking an extra point, so why do it if the benefit is basically the same as kicking the easier extra point? The two-point try failed when the Ikeville team gang-tackled poor Neil.

Another time, Jonasburg had the ball at the Ikeville thirty-yard line and it was fourth down with two yards to go. Coach Williams had a choice: punt or go for it. He decided to punt, giving the ball back to Ikeville. Julio Haberberg, a shaggy-haired kid whose sister rode my bus, jogged onto the field. He took the snap and booted the ball—into the end zone. So Ikeville got the ball on the twenty-yard line and eventually scored seven plays later.

Again, I disagreed with Coach W.'s choice. If Jonasburg had gone for it on fourth down, they might have kept the drive alive and had a chance to score. Coach W. was probably worried about not getting the two yards on fourth down and having to give the ball back to Ikeville. But by punting the ball he gave it back to them anyway. And only ten yards farther down the field than if he had tried and failed on fourth down. It seemed like Coach W. gave up a huge opportunity—trying to keep the ball and score—for a small cost of possibly giving the ball back to Ikeville, which he did anyway by punting!

At halftime, I walked with Ben Barnes to the

concession stand, where I ordered a pretzel and a large lemonade. Ben was tall and skinny and on the basketball team, and he ate the kind of stuff my mom would faint if she saw on my plate. Sure enough, he ordered something called an "Indiana taco." It was a bag of corn chips that someone had opened up and filled with a heaping scoopful of beef, topped with cheese and sour cream.

"Hey, health nuts," came a voice from behind us.

As I spun around, I could feel my face breaking into a smile.

"Hi, Jamie," I said. "How you doin'?"

"I'd be doing better," she said, "if Coach Williams had remembered to turn his brain on. What's he thinking out there? Or, better yet, is he thinking?"

Amazing.

We had thought exactly the same thing. Other kids and parents were buzzing about how well Ikeville was playing or complaining about the Jonasburg quarterback. Jamie and I were the only ones to realize that Coach Williams wasn't helping.

"He should put lipstick on his head and make up his mind," she said.

"Huh?"

"Get it? Lipstick? Make up his mind. Makeup?"

"Ugh," I said. "That's a lame one."

"Why didn't he go for it on fourth down?" yelled Jamie. "I mean, you knew that Julio would kick it as hard as he could and end up sending it into the end zone. He might as well have just handed them the ball."

"I know! And how about that two-point conversion call?" I exclaimed.

"Don't get me started," said Jamie. "We would only have been down by six points, and if he had gone for it on fourth like he should have, we would probably be ahead by one point at halftime instead of down by two touchdowns!"

I nodded. And even though we were losing, I couldn't help but smile.

In the end, Jonasburg lost 33–20. At some point Coach Williams got so frustrated he threw his clipboard into the air. Like most of his team's passes, it hit the ground and bounced harmlessly away.

———

The day after the game, Kevin and I both helped out Mom and Dad at the store. We painted a back wall and swept the floors and threw out broken shards of clay. Mom sold a painting in the morning, and Dad sold two flowerpots in the afternoon. Before Kevin ran off to a movie with his new flock of friends, Dad suggested we celebrate a successful day by having dinner as a family.

"Good idea," Mom said. "What do you guys want us to cook?"

Mom and Dad took turns cooking dinner. It was a lot of tofu and salad and dishes our friends called "Hippie Food." But, probably because we grew up eating it, Kevin and I never complained much. Actually, I bet most kids would prefer tofu to chicken fingers—which always sound gross to me—if they had a blind taste test.

Before I could think about what to request, Dad piped up. "No cooking! We're going *out* to eat tonight."

Going to a restaurant as a family? We hadn't done that in a long time. Even when we drove halfway across the country to Indiana, Mom and

Dad didn't want us to eat fast food. Instead we'd find a local grocery store and make sandwiches in the car.

"Why not?" Mom said. "I could use a night out. And, anyway, we should be celebrating."

Celebrating? I ran through everyone's birthday in my head, making sure I hadn't forgotten.

"Celebrating what?" I asked.

"How well it's going for all of us in Indiana," Mom said. "This was a big move. It was a real test for the whole family, and we're passing with flying colors."

I smiled a little as we got in the car. It was nice to see that Mom wasn't worrying about me anymore.

We ended up at Grisani's, which claimed to have "The Finest Italian Cuisine in Jonasburg," not bothering to add that it was also the *only* Italian cuisine in the town. As we studied our menus, I must have made a funny face.

"What is it, Mitch?" Dad asked.

"I don't get it," I said. "Why write on the menu 'a heaping portion of delicious pasta'?"

"That's what I was going to order," Mom said. "What could possibly be wrong with that?"

"I'm sure nothing's wrong with the food," I said. "But why not just call it a plate of pasta and then serve me a lot, which would be a good surprise. When you call it 'heaping,' my expectations are going to be high. Then you add on 'delicious.' If my definitions of heaping and delicious aren't their definitions of heaping and delicious, I'm going to be disappointed."

"If you can't eat it all, bring the rest home in a doggie bag," said Kevin, missing the point, as usual.

But Mom got it. "That's true, Mitch. I guess I do expect something really good."

"And the description made her want to order it, too. Isn't that what a restaurant should do?" my dad asked.

"No," I said. "A restaurant wants you to come back. If your order is disappointing, then you probably won't."

Everybody went back to their menus, but I hoped this idea would somehow stick in my parents' heads when they went to their art store in the morning. Sometimes they describe the pieces in it as "beautiful" or "picturesque" or "scenic," but if the customer doesn't see them that way, they're not going to buy anything or tell their friends about the store. I wish my parents understood these things better, since it was a big part of why we had to move in the first place. But we were having such a nice time that I decided to let it go.

On Sunday, I did my homework in the morning so I could be sure to watch the Baltimore-Pittsburgh game in the afternoon. Ordinarily, I would have just enjoyed the game. But I got an extra surge of excitement knowing that I had bragging rights with Jamie—and five bucks—resting on the outcome. For most of the game, Pittsburgh was leading. My grin must have been pretty obvious.

"What are you so happy about?" said Kevin. "I thought you didn't like Pittsburgh."

"I like them today," I said.

"Let me guess," said Kevin. "You have a bunch of their players on your fantasy league team."

"Nope," I said. "Not a single one."

"Then you bet money on them with another boy."

Was it that obvious?

"Something like that," I said, deciding not to tell Kevin that he was right about the betting, but that the "boy" was Jamie.

"And you took Pittsburgh?"

"How could I not? I saw online that both of Baltimore's best wide receivers *and* their starting linebacker wouldn't be playing. And that when they play road games against passing teams, they usually lose. Especially when the field is natural grass and not turf."

"Isn't that kinda cheating?" asked Kevin.

"It's not cheating," I said, staring at him. "It's called having more information. That's all."

"It doesn't seem fair. You're kind of taking advantage. And isn't this *exactly* the kind of thing that got you in trouble in California?" Kevin asked.

"Whatever," I shot back. "You wouldn't understand."

"I'm just saying," said Kevin in a *see what I care?* voice. "I wouldn't be happy if a friend did that to me."

We watched the rest of the game. Baltimore made a comeback and tied it up in the fourth quarter. On the next kickoff, the return man for Pittsburgh fumbled. Suddenly, with less than two minutes left to play, Baltimore had a chance to win. After a few running plays, they let the game clock bleed down, and then the field-goal kicker came on with just a few seconds left.

As if he were guiding the ball with a remote control, he drilled a perfect kick between the two uprights. Baltimore won, 30–27, and their fans in the stadium went nuts. The announcers called it "arguably the best game of the season so far." Kevin was standing up and pumping his fist. Then he looked over at me, confused. "How come you're still smiling?" he asked. "In case you didn't notice, your team just lost."

"True," I said. "But for me to lose my bet, Baltimore had to win by at least four points."

Kevin shook his head. "You're sneaky," he said, "but you're good. There should be a word for that."

Hopefully it's not "annoying," I thought to myself.

As the television coverage went back to the studio,

Kevin flopped down on the couch. "I don't get it, Mitch. I never have any allowance left at the end of the week, but you have money just lying around to bet on football."

"You look at your allowance the wrong way," I said. "You think of it as money you found. Like, *'Hey, here's thirty-five dollars Mom and Dad gave me! Sweet. I'm going to buy a video game, go to the movies, and spend the rest on iTunes.'* But it's not money they gave you. It's money you earned. You got it for doing your chores."

"So?"

"So it's payment you got for doing work. You took out the trash. You mowed the yard. You're going to rake the leaves this fall. Remember that and you're going to spend it more carefully than if you think of it as lucky money you stumble on every week."

Kevin thought about it. "It's like I'm a worker getting paid thirty-five dollars, not a guy who won thirty-five dollars in one of those scratch-off games they always advertise on TV?"

"Exactly!" I said. "Lottery winners use their

money to go on cruises and buy new golf clubs and fur coats and stuff they don't need. Workers use their money to buy groceries and things they *need*. And hopefully they save some, too, for when other stuff comes up."

"Maybe in a few days you can help me make some picks for next Sunday's game. I want to do some gambling, too."

"Sure," I said.

"One more thing," he said. "How many enemies have you made since we've moved here?"

"None," I shot back. "What are you trying to say?"

"Just be careful, little brother," he said. "It's only stupid money, you know?"

Only stupid money? Sometimes I can't believe Kevin and I came from the same set of parents.

CHAPTER 5

KA-CHING!

It was early in the year, but I already had a favorite teacher. If my school hours were one of those stock market charts showing "highs" and "lows" then my day hits its peak when I sit in third-period math with Mr. Rafferty. I wouldn't exactly call him "cool." (In fact, he's definitely not cool.) It looks like his hair is afraid of his forehead and is backing away as fast as it can. When he walks around the classroom, his shoes squeak. His arms are so hairy, it seems like they're carpeted.

But he's one of those teachers who make class so fun that you forget you're learning. Today he taught us about percentages, fractions, and decimal points, and he used baseball as an example. "When a batter hits .300, it's not really 'three hundred' the way the announcers say," he said to the class. "It's .300 or .3 or thirty percent or three out of ten."

My hand shot up. "The difference is that three-for-ten in baseball is good. But three-for-ten on a test is a big fat F!"

Mr. Rafferty smiled. "Good point, Mitch." Then he waited for a beat.

"Get it?" he said. "Good point. Decimal point? A joke? Anyone?"

There were a few groans. I've always wondered why adults don't realize that if you have to explain your joke, maybe—just maybe—it wasn't funny to begin with.

When I got back to my locker, Jamie was waiting for me. She was wearing a backward baseball cap, a Jonasburg sweatshirt, jeans—and a nasty frown.

"Here you go," she said, throwing a crumpled five-dollar bill at me.

I felt bad. But not bad enough to reject it. As I put the money in my pocket, she kept staring lasers at me.

"What?" I said.

"You know what," she said. "Three of Baltimore's best players were hurt and didn't even play!"

"Maybe," I said. "I can't remember."

"Yeah, right. That's the last time I make a bet with you."

"There's no rule against having more information," I said.

"Don't you think you should have told me that Baltimore was going to be fielding a JV team?"

"Then you wouldn't have taken the bet."

"But at least then," she said, arching an eyebrow, "we'd still be friends."

An awkward silence hung in the air like a bad smell. Uh-oh. I got a little jump in my stomach, like I had ruined a good thing.

Then she smiled. "I'm just playing with you."

I wonder if she heard me exhale with relief.

"Don't worry," she told me. "I'll get you back."

She made a fist, and we pounded knuckles.

As usual, I sat by Ben Barnes at lunch. As usual, he was already eating when I got there. And as usual, he was eating the kind of food my parents call "poison," tearing through a bag of chips and a pack of cookies while draining a can of fruit punch. Plus, he bought a double order of Tater Tots on the hot-lunch line. Ben scrunched up his face as he stabbed at one with his fork.

"You okay?" I asked.

"Yeah, but these Tater Tots are awful. I don't know how you manage to spoil Tater Tots, but they did it."

"Then why are you eating them?"

"Duh," he said, shaking his head. "Because I paid for 'em. A dollar fifty."

"Would you eat them if they were on my tray and I just gave you some for free?"

"No way!"

"That makes no sense, then," I said. "If you paid for the Tater Tots, the money is gone. Why make it worse by making yourself eat something you don't want?"

"Maybe you're right, Mitch." Of course I was right. But by then he had put the last of the Tater Tots in his mouth.

"Hey," he said. At least I think it was "hey." I couldn't tell for sure, since his mouth was full. "I want to bet on a football game, too."

"What?" I said.

"Like you did with Jamie," he mumbled between bites.

"How'd you hear about that?"

"Everyone knows," he said with a shrug. "You won five bucks from Jamie betting on football."

Note to self: Rumors and gossip travel the halls here faster than a racecar—a word that spells itself backward, by the way—at the Indianapolis 500.

"So?" said Ben.

"So what?"

"Can I make a bet with you?" he asked.

"No. Well, I guess. Okay. What?"

"I love the Colts. They're playing Denver this weekend, and I know they're going to kill them."

Ka-ching, I thought to myself. He's betting on the Colts not because he knows anything about the game, but because they're his favorite team. I smelled opportunity. I smelled money. He would bet with his heart. I would bet with my head.

"Sure," I said, trying to sound reluctant. "I guess I'll take Denver, but to make it fair, how about the Colts have to win by at least six points?"

"Six points!" said Ben. "Heck, that's barely a touchdown. They're going to win by two or three touchdowns! You can make it ten points if you want."

Even better! Ben thought the Colts were going to crush Denver because the Colts were his favorite team. But I knew the truth. The Colts were at best an even match with Denver, and winning at all, let alone by ten points, would be pretty unlikely. This was an easy bet.

It was right around then that the idea hit me. I could bet my classmates on football and take advantage of (1) their being die-hard fans, which could get in the way of their judgment, and (2) me having more information. But even then, there would be cases when I could lose. A star on my team could get injured unexpectedly. The officials could make a bad call. Someone could have as much information as me. For whatever reason, my team might just stink one Sunday. There could be all sorts of flukes.

But what if I could eliminate the risk? Then I could make money without worrying about losing it!

It was an incredible idea, and now all I needed was a willing partner.

———

"So here's how it works," I said.

Jamie looked hard at me, and I couldn't tell if she was skeptical—after all, she had just lost five dollars to me—or if she was intrigued.

"You collect the bets for one team. I collect bets for the other team. Ten bucks a bet. Winner gets eighteen. We get two for our services."

"What service is that?" she asked.

"We're arranging all the bets," I explained. "If we didn't do this, no one would even have a chance to make money."

"What do you mean?"

"It's like a salad bar at a grocery store," I said. "You could buy the lettuce and the carrots and the cucumber and make your own salad. But that would take a long time. So you go to the salad bar. It's more expensive, but you're willing to pay extra because they've done the work for you, right? The lettuce is already washed. The carrots are peeled. The cucumber is chopped. And it's all right there in front of you. So you're willing to pay more."

She nodded. "But what if everyone wants to bet on one team and no one wants to bet on the other team?"

"This," I said, "is where the genius of Mitch kicks in. We only take bets if we know we can line up the same amount of people on each side. The Broncos play the Colts this Sunday. If ten people want to bet on the Broncos, we find ten people to take the Colts."

"Ten bets on the Broncos. Ten bets on the Colts. And we get two dollars a bet, so we get twenty dollars no matter what happens, no matter who wins." Jamie's face suddenly lit with a smile. "Not bad."

"Thanks," I said, smiling.

"But wait a minute," she said. "What if we can't find ten people to bet on the Broncos? This is Colts country, you know."

"That's where we set points," I responded. "Just like our bet last week. You had to beat the Steelers by more than four points, remember?" I can't help taunting her a little.

"Yeah," she said a little bitterly.

"We offer points to people to get them to bet on the Broncos. Maybe they think the Colts will win, but not by more than ten points. So, we say Broncos plus ten points. That's how they do it in Vegas."

"Yeah, okay, that's pretty clever," she said. "But the Colts winning by ten over Denver is crazy. No one is nuts enough to think they're going to win by that much!"

I smiled, thinking of Ben. "I don't know. People can get carried away with this stuff." I was so excited I was having trouble sitting still. "So are you in?"

"Let me think about it."

"For how long?"

She scowled at me. "For as long as I feel like it, Mitch."

I didn't mind waiting. I was psyched. She liked my idea, we were still friends, and we were about to make some money together. "Okay, okay, fine. Hey, can I ask you a question while you think about it?"

"Shoot," she said.

"How'd you get so into sports, anyway? Don't take this the wrong way, but I've never met a girl who..."

"Who what? Would rather play football than do her nails?" she said in the girliest voice ever.

"Yeah," I said. "Something like that."

"Well, my dad is a big sports fan, and he got me into it. Once, we were watching a football game and he said to me, 'Having you around is as good as having a son.' It probably slipped out. But after that, I couldn't disappoint him by asking to get a manicure or bake muffins or something girly like that."

"But you do *like* sports, right?" I said.

"Oh, sure, totally," she said. "I might not have tried them without my dad, but after a while I realized I loved them. Sports are way more fun that all that girly crap other girls do. Okay, buddy. Your turn."

"Huh? My turn to do what?"

"Answer a question. What did you mean when you said you got your head dunked in a toilet at your old school? What was that about?"

"Oh. Yeah." I didn't want to talk about that day so much. But Jamie had just told me the thing with her dad. So I kind of felt like I owed her, and I did feel kind of bad about the bet and all.

"My other school, back in California...I don't know. I wasn't exactly popular." I shrugged.

I could tell she was getting ready to give me some trash talk—

You, not popular? I can't believe it—but then I think she saw my face. "Go on," she said, and she even sounded a little sorry.

I didn't tell her all of it. I'd never really told anybody all of it. Elbows to the ribs. Books knocked out of my hands. Kids scrambling as soon as I was about to open up my locker so they could slam it closed and I couldn't grab a book or a pen.

"So there was a bunch of eighth graders on the basketball team," I told Jamie. "And they grabbed me one day and decided to give me a swirly. Stuck my head in the toilet and flushed. You know, so your hair looks like a Dairy Queen cone, all swirly."

"That sucks," Jamie said angrily. "Why didn't you tell a teacher?"

"I *did*."

That was the worst part, actually. I'd told Mr. Funkle, our assistant principal. And do you know what he said?

What did you do this time, Mitch?

He'd practically sung it, rolling his eyes and tapping a pen against the coffee mug he always carried around. After I'd explained what happened, he told me he'd take my complaint "under advisement," whatever that meant. I think it was adultspeak for "I have more important things to do than deal with you and your wet hair, kid."

"That sucks!" Jamie said again, really mad. I hadn't wanted to tell her, but I have to admit I kind of liked seeing her get all fired up about something that happened to me six months ago. "I can't believe that! I can't—wait a minute. Mitch?"

"What?"

"What *did* you do?"

"Hey! Nothing!"

She held up her hands. "I'm not saying you deserved it, dude. Seriously, nobody deserves that. They should have expelled all those kids and fired that principal. I'm on your side. But...maybe there was...something? Some reason they were mad at you?"

"Hey, I'm the victim here. I didn't do anything!"

"Seriously?"

"Well...okay. Fine. I did kind of take some money from Carl Lake."

Carl was probably the tallest kid at my old school. He was lanky and had this mop of hair that made him look like a toothbrush. He had been taking lunch money from sixth graders the past week, and one day it was my turn.

"Got any lunch money, kid?" he said in the deepest voice he could make.

I could tell he was trying to scare me, and that he thought I was just some little sixth-grade idiot that he could step all over. But I could also tell he wasn't going to leave empty-handed, not quietly anyway.

"I don't have any money," I said. "Because I used it all to buy these candy bars." I showed him the box of twenty candy bars I had, which I was supposed to sell for my computer club.

"You gonna eat all those?" he sneered. "Maybe I'll help you!" And he grabbed the box of candy from me.

"No," I laughed, trying to stay calm, "I was going to sell them."

"To who?" he asked.

"Yeah, I bought these candy bars because I thought I could sell them during lunch or between classes. Figured I could make about twenty-five cents on every bar."

He had already opened one of them and was munching away on it, but I could see I had his attention.

"In fact," I continued, "maybe you'd be interested in helping me sell them. We'd split the profits, of course."

It was risky. Carl could have easily just taken the candy bars away from me, but given the amount of money I'd seen him collect this week from other kids, I suspected he wanted the money more than the candy.

"Can you get more?" he asked.

"Sure," I said, "and if you want to partner with me, you can cover the seventh and eighth graders. They won't take the candy from *you!*"

Carl smiled. I think he liked the thought of other kids not daring to steal from him. "Okay," he said, grinning, "but I get twenty cents. You can keep five."

It was a pretty lopsided partnership. But, figuring this might happen, I had a better plan. You see, for the kid in the computer club who sold the most candy bars, there was a fifty-dollar prize. Carl would probably manage to sell at least five boxes or a hundred candy bars, netting him a profit of twenty dollars. I would get five dollars. But, since I would be the one who sold the most, I also got the fifty-dollar prize, which Carl didn't know about.

Unfortunately, he eventually found out about the prize from his younger brother, who was also in the sixth grade. Carl wasn't too happy.

I told this to Jamie, and she shook her head.

"What did you do with the money, Mitch?" she asked.

"I gave some of it back to the kids whose lunch money was stolen," I said, "then kept the rest. But I probably would've given it all back to avoid that swirly."

"I'm going to have to think twice before I go into business with you," she said.

———

"What the heck is that?" I asked Ben Barnes. By the time I got to the lunch table the next day, his mouth was already filled with food. Food I had a hard time identifying.

"What? You mean you've never seen a tender-loin sandwich before?" he said incredulously.

"Nuh-uh."

I looked closely at the lunch that he'd spread out on his cafeteria tray. It seemed to be a piece of fried meat, flattened until it was the size of a small pizza, and tucked into a bun. He told me it was some sort of Indiana specialty, like sourdough in San Francisco.

"It's pretty good," he said. "Try some if you want."

He ripped off a corner and handed it me. I looked at it with suspicion but figured if it was poison, well, a lot of other kids were going to be sick besides me.

"Not bad," I said.

"That's it?" said Ben.

"Okay, it's good." I kept chewing. "Really good. So good, I'll be right back. I'm going to get one now."

I came back from the lunch line, and it happened. I'm not sure how. It kinda just did. As I started to unwrap my tenderloin, Ben was slurping the last bit of his milk through his straw—I hate that sound—and was getting ready to leave. Seth Brockman had already left and Trevor Wiseman was out with the stomach flu. At the table behind us, a knot of girls was getting up together, all except Jamie, who was still eating. Two bites into my tenderloin, she and I were the only two people left in our corner of the cafeteria. It was like we broke the tribal rules of the cafeteria but obeyed the rules of gravity. We scooted our chairs over and sat together.

"Hey," I said.

"You gonna eat that slop?" she said, looking at my sandwich. "I wouldn't feed that to my dog."

"It's really good," I said, shrugging and continuing to eat.

"Good to see you have the same standards for your food as you have for your football teams."

"Speaking of football, have you given any thought to my idea?"

Jamie started to smile. "Wellllllllll, Mitchell—"

"Mitch," I corrected her. I couldn't let that one slip, even if she was about to deliver good news.

"Sorry." She paused. "Okay, I admit you're onto something."

"Oh yeah?"

"Because I just mentioned, real casually, that if

people wanted to bet ten dollars on the Colts beating the Broncos, I might be able to help. Avni Garg was the first. Then Jonah Gideon said he would—"

"How many total?"

"Ten so far!" she said. "And I barely tried."

"Did you explain to them if they bet ten dollars and won, they would get eighteen back?"

"Yeah, nobody cared," she said. "They're so confident their team's going to win, it doesn't matter to them."

"Here's the crazy thing," I said. "I already have ten people willing to bet ten dollars on the Broncos. You know what this means?"

"Yeah," she said. "We're going to make twenty bucks no matter which team wins!"

"And you know what else? This is only one game! Why don't we do this for the Vikings-Packers, the Dolphins-Jets, the—"

"Slow down, slow down. Don't get greedy," she warned.

"It's not greed. It's opportunity."

"Let's just do one game this week and see how it goes. Make sure we didn't overlook something."

She got up to bus her tray, but I wasn't done with my sandwich.

What should I do now? Shake Jamie's hand like we were real businesspeople making an agreement? Give her a high five? Bump fists? I panicked and just sort of tapped her elbow.

Awkward.

Of course, that had to be the time Zander McCallum walked by.

"Who's this," he said, pointing to Jamie standing next to me, "your girlfriend?"

I wanted to say, *Even better—my business partner.*

But for some reason it was like the words got stuck at a traffic light that had turned red. The only thing that came into my brain sputtered out.

"Um, uh, nah, no," I stammered. "We're just friends."

"Sure you are," said Zander. "Suuuuure you are."

CHAPTER 6

RISKY BUSINESS

And a little something extra for you off the top.

When Sunday rolled around and it was time to watch football, Kevin was in a foul mood. He had twisted his ankle in the football game on Friday and spent the weekend limping around and popping Tylenol like they were candy. If I had a dollar for every time Mom said, "Keep that foot elevated, Kevin," I would be rich. Adding insult to injury—literally—Kevin's team was still lousy. Their record was 0–2, and no one could figure out why they weren't better. Jonasburg had some good players, including Kevin. There were a lot of seniors who had played as juniors last season, so they couldn't blame inexperience. Everyone liked Coach Williams, even if some of his decisions didn't make much sense.

"I don't get it. We should be so much better than we are," Kevin complained over dinner. "We're never going to beat Clarksville in the Corncob Bowl."

"Who's that?" Dad asked.

"Duh," Kevin shot back. "Only our biggest rivals."

"And beat them in the what?" Dad said. "The Corn something?"

"It's the Corncob Bowl, Dad," Kevin said in his *you're driving me crazy* voice. "Only the most important game we play every year. It's always the last game of the season and it's a huge deal."

"Sorry," Dad said. "I'm new in town. Unlike you, old-timer." That was Dad's way of scolding Kevin without really scolding him. Dad was smart like that. "Hey," he went on. "I have an idea: Maybe you could have Mitch study statistics or something and use that to help the team."

Kevin started laughing, shooting me a look

that said *can you believe how clueless our dad is?* "It's not like we're losing because we don't have a ninety-pound middle-school dweeb to help us," he chortled.

"Kevin," Mom started in, but he quickly interrupted.

"I know, I know, but really, come on!" He laughed again.

I didn't even mind Kevin calling me a dweeb. But I did mind when he said this: "I wish we had Clint Grayson on our team to kick and punt. Do you know him, Mitch?"

"Yeah, I know him," I said. "He treats me like a piece of dirt. Why do you even have to mention his name?"

"Because with that bionic leg of his, he might help us win a game."

———

So maybe I was a ninety-pound middle-school dweeb. But I was on my way to being a rich ninety-pound middle-school dweeb. I had a wad of twenty ten-dollar bills—two hundred dollars!—in my sock drawer. And no matter what happened in the Colts-Broncos game, I only had to give one hundred and eighty of it back (and ten to Jamie).

"Let me guess," Kevin said as we were settling in to watch the game together. "You have a bet on this game, too."

"Yup."

"Who do you want to win?" he said. "Or lose, so long as it's not by too many points?"

"Don't care."

"What do you mean?"

"I like the Colts better," I explained, slowing down for effect.

"But..."

"But I win either way. I got rid of all the risk. Eliminated it." I smirked.

"You did what?"

"I found ten kids who wanted to bet ten dollars to take the Colts. And ten who bet ten dollars to take the Broncos. The winners get eighteen dollars, and I get two dollars for each bet," I said all this in my best *do I have to explain everything?* tone.

He paused, and I could tell he was thinking it through.

"So you get two dollars just for being, like, the middleman. No matter what happens."

"Exactly."

"Pretty smart, Mitch," he said. "Pretty smart."

We sat in silence, watching the game for a few minutes before Kevin spoke up again. "If you can make money without any risk, how come you're just doing it for one game? Why not do it for all the games?"

I slapped my magazine on the coffee table. "Exactly!" I said. "That's exactly what I said to Jamie!"

"Who's that?" Kevin asked.

Darn! I let it slip out. "Just a kid at school," I said quietly. I had to change the subject before he could ask another question about Jamie. I was just thankful she had a name that worked for boys as well as girls. "Hey, is your foot elevated?"

"Shut up."

———

The Colts beat the Broncos, 34–28. Not that I really cared. I had made the easiest twenty dollars of my life. And more was coming. Ben owed me five dollars, too, since the Colts only won by six, not the ten points he'd bet.

There was one small hitch. I had to give eighteen dollars to the ten classmates who had won. That meant that I needed a lot of one-dollar and five-dollar bills. If I tried to get them from Mom and Dad, they might ask too many questions. I didn't have a bank account, so I couldn't just run to the local credit union, which was next to my parents' store.

Then I got an idea. I would go to Irma, the cafeteria cashier. It might be kind of weird. I mean, why would a seventh grader need to make so much change? But I trusted myself to smooth-talk her.

When Dad dropped me off at school, I went to the cafeteria to buy a cinnamon roll. I approached Irma with the biggest smile I could make.

"Hi, Irma," I said, remembering that I once read that successful people in business always try to address others by their name. "How was your weekend, Irma?"

"Great. I took my grandkids to the mall in Louisville, and we went to the zoo."

"I haven't been to that one, since we just moved here and all. But the zoo where I used to live in San Francisco had an amazing penguin-feeding area. Do they have that over in Louisville?"

"Oh, yeah," said Irma. "A great gorilla exhibit and giraffe feeding, too."

This was another trick I learned from one of those business shows. Small talk = big talk. Just having a normal, simple conversation can help put people at ease before you ask for what you really want.

"Here's eighty cents for the world's best cinnamon roll," I said.

When she handed me back two dimes, I had a response ready. "Keep the change!"

"Oh, I can't do that, Mitch."

"But your service is the best!" I said, still trying to turn on the charm.

"Thanks, hon," she said. "But I can't."

"Oh, one more thing, Irma," I said casually. "I almost forgot: Do you think that if I gave you eighty dollars in tens, you could change it for me and I could get ten fives, and thirty ones?"

"Um..."

"It's for a class project," I explained, quickly convincing myself that I was not *technically* lying. (What? It was for people in my class. And it was for a project. A business project I was doing with Jamie. Who's also in my class. See? Class project.)

"Well, this one time, I guess," she said, clearly uneasy, but not so uneasy that she didn't do it. She fumbled in a drawer of the cash register and counted the money, looking over her shoulder. As she handed me the bills, the mood had changed. It was like the warmth was gone and suddenly there was a frost. But I got what I wanted. I felt like a real businessman, closing a deal.

When I walked down the hall to go to my locker, I was hoping Jamie would already be there and we could—quietly—celebrate our success. But I couldn't see her because my view was blocked by a pack of kids. At first I thought it was a fight and everyone had formed a circle to watch. Then I realized they were there for *me*. It was the ten winners who had come to collect their money. Good thing I got those singles from Irma.

"Yeah, Colts!" an eighth grader I'd never seen before yelped, slapping five with everyone standing around. "Now where's the rookie bookie with my money?"

The Rookie Bookie? Did I (finally) have a nickname that wasn't making fun of me? So awesome!

I got out the sheet of paper Jamie had copied for me with all the names and the bets. One by one, I started to pay the winners. As I crossed off their names, I reminded them that they had a chance to double their money the following Sunday. Midway through, out of the corner of my eye, I saw Mr. Rafferty watching our group.

I didn't know of any *specific* rule against organizing some bets. I mean, it's not like it had come up at assembly or something. *Say no to drugs. Stay in school. And don't start a career as a bookie between classes.*

And what was wrong with it, really? I wasn't making anybody do anything they didn't want to do. I wasn't lying, or stealing money like Carl Lake had at my old school. And everybody was lining up at *my* locker. Everybody wanted to talk to me! Me, the kid who'd had his head in a toilet six months ago.

But I still didn't want Mr. Rafferty to see what was going on. As he started walking toward my locker, I rotated my body so my back was to him and tucked all the football sheets into the folder I was holding.

"Mitch," he said firmly. "I can only assume you're talking to everyone about the excitement of fractions." Luckily, he kept walking.

When the crowd finally thinned out, I saw Jamie. "Here's your share for all that hard work," I said, handing her a ten-dollar bill.

"You're right," she said, staring at a piece of paper.

"Right about what?"

"This coming Sunday, why limit ourselves to one game?"

Yes! She had warmed up to the idea.

"I circled five games for us to target, ten bets on each side," she said, sounding very businesslike. "I like making ten bucks without taking any risks. But I like making fifty bucks even more."

"So what's the plan?"

"Here's the game schedule I printed out," she said, adjusting the black baseball cap she was wearing. "You find ten people who want to bet on each team playing at home. I find ten people who want to bet on each team playing on the road. That way we won't get confused."

I liked the way this girl thought.

"You know, Avni Garg loves the Dolphins," I said. "Target kids like that first, offering them their favorite team. They use their feelings—not common sense—when it comes to their team. Classic mistake. Doesn't matter how bad the Dolphins are. Avni will always bet on them. Same for Drew Scott and Ben with the Colts, Raffi Cody with the Patriots—"

"Okay, I get it."

"Plan?" I said.

"Plan."

Nothing like a strategy meeting with your business partner to start the day. We knocked knuckles and went to class.

CHAPTER 7

WORD OF MOUTH

People in business are always talking about "word of mouth." When someone talks about your store or your restaurant or your amusement park or whatever, that's the best kind of advertising. And there's no better place for "word of mouth" than the halls of a middle school. All these people under one roof? Gossip and rumors travel at Mach 3.

So I shouldn't have been surprised when a line had formed near my locker and there was a mob of kids surrounding it waiting for the "Rookie Bookie" and "Mitch the new kid" to take their football bets. It had taken precisely two class periods for "word of mouth" to spread throughout the entire school.

I took everyone's ten dollars and made a mark next to what team they wanted. At one point I looked over my shoulder and saw Jamie at her locker. Our eyes met. She winked at me. I guess this is what it feels like to be popular.

"Why don't you just pay me now?" Noah Raymond said, smiling.

"Why's that?" I said.

"Because it's beyond obvious that Chicago is going to beat Atlanta."

"We'll see," I said, taking his money and checking his name. "Actually, you're probably right," I added. I wanted him to keep betting after all.

"Hey, I know you're Mitch, but I don't think we've really met," said a seventh grader with a buzz cut, his hair standing straight up like freshly mowed grass. "I'm Max. You sure've brought, like, an exciting vibe with you. Is that how they would say it in California?"

"Yeah, sure. I guess. Thanks," I said, trying quickly to think of what a cool California kid might say. "Thanks, dude...man." Ugh. Awkward.

"Okay. Go, Dolphins!" said Max. "Catch you later, dude-man."

Maybe not so awkward?

It went on like that until I took the last bet. By the time the bell sounded, I had five hundred dollars bulging in my pocket. Assuming Jamie did her job and found people to make bets on the other side, we were in business. Serious business.

In Mr. Rafferty's class, we were still studying percentages. Standing in front of the class, he looked like a mad scientist from a horror movie. What was left of his hair was shooting in all sorts of different directions, like he had put his finger in an electrical socket. His shirt had a giant crease in it. His wool pants looked like they had been made of leftover fabric from the drapes, and I noticed that his belt had bypassed one of the loops. I didn't care. He was such an awesome teacher.

"...so a fraction can also be expressed as a percent," he was saying. "If there are twenty-four of you in the class and twelve of you get A's on the test, what percent gets A's?" he asked.

A few hands shot up. Mr. Rafferty ignored them.

"Gabby, want to try it?" he asked, pointing at a girl in the front row who seemed really shy. She hardly ever talked, and she walked around with her head down. Now she didn't answer.

"We can do this, Gabby!" Mr. Rafferty said cheerfully. "Can you reduce twelve over twenty-four?"

"Half," she mumbled.

"Right!" Mr. Rafferty practically shouted. "And what percent is half?"

"Fifty?" Gabby said meekly.

"You got it!" Mr. Rafferty gushed. "Fifty percent will get A's. And I bet you'll be one of them, Gabby."

Even as she tucked her head, I could tell she was smiling.

"Okay, time for another one," said Mr. Rafferty.

"Let's say Mitch has been going to a new school for twenty days. He's been a great kid for nineteen days. On one of the days, he made an error in judgment and did something he shouldn't."

The class giggled and looked at me. I smiled. It was pretty cool Mr. R. was using me as an example, but I also got kind of a funny feeling in my stomach.

"What percent of the days has Mitch made the wrong choice?"

Okay, I got it. This was Mr. Rafferty's way of warning me: *I don't know exactly what you're up to, but I know you're doing something you shouldn't be doing.*

But as the rest of the class was figuring out what percent of my days at Jonasburg had been spent making wrong choices, I was still thinking about making more money. I had five hundred dollars in my pocket, and Jamie and I were going to get to keep—here you go, Mr. Rafferty—ten percent of it. So fifty dollars was going to be ours. And, if Jamie also got five hundred dollars in bets, that's one hundred dollars in total. Fifty for me, fifty for her.

Fifty dollars!

And this was only the beginning.

Jamie and I were on our way.

━━━

While Jamie and I had figured out a way not to lose at football, the Jonasburg High football team wasn't so fortunate. Even against teams that were clearly weaker, they kept putting up the smaller numbers on the scoreboard. In one game, they were winning easily going into the fourth quarter, but then gave up three touchdowns. In another game, they lost 13–12 because their kicker, Tom Denzel, missed a field goal. ("Clint Grayson could have made that kick," said Kevin.)

The worst, though, came in a game against the Verona Vipers. Late in the game, Jonasburg was hanging on to a slim lead, the way you hang on to the rail of a roller coaster. Verona was marching down the field with a chance to win. But then Nathan Isaac— one of the seniors who sometimes drove Kevin home from school—made a fantastic interception.

The crowd went crazy. Finally, victory was at hand.

Nathan had caught the ball and was hit at the same time by two players, spinning him around. He kept his balance and started to run. But there was this one problem.

In his excitement, he had run down the field in the wrong direction.

Maybe it was because he'd heard all the cheers. Maybe it was because he was disoriented from the collision with the other players. Not only that, but the louder everyone yelled "Nooooo!!" the more it seemed to encourage him. In what was only a few seconds, he scored for the other team.

NOOOO-OOOO!

When he crossed into the end zone, he did a somersault, congratulating himself.

Nathan probably wondered why he wasn't mobbed by teammates, the way it usually happens when a player scores a touchdown, especially a dramatic one late in the game. When the other Jonasburg players arrived downfield and explained what had happened, Nathan stomped his foot, put both hands on his helmet and...well, wait. Why I am explaining this to you? You can see it all for yourself. Just search for the video called "Jonas-burg Wrong Way Touchdown" online. When I last checked, there were more than 1.7 million views.

After that game, Kevin didn't really seem all that upset. He seemed sort of confused and shocked, like when you wake up in the backseat of a car and aren't sure where you are. *Huh? Wha—? What just happened? Where are we?*

The next morning, he was still trying to make sense of it all. "We had that game *won*," he complained. "I mean, it was *over*. O-ver."

"Maybe your team is just cursed," I said. For the record, I don't believe in curses. But they seem to make people feel better. It's like: *Nothing can be anyone's fault or anyone's responsibility if there's a curse.* It puts the blame on, like, this supernatural force, not on anyone specific. Maybe that would make Kevin feel better.

Or not.

"It's not that," said Kevin. "But all this losing has become like a disease that has gotten contagious. The tacklers tackle a little worse. The kickers kick a little worse. The coaches coach a little worse. The bus driver gets lost on the way to every game. Even the cheerleaders forget their cheers and can't balance on their pyramids."

"Maybe that's the first problem," said Dad, overhearing. "You need to stop paying attention to the cheerleaders during the games. I know they're foxy and all, but wait till after the game, would ya?"

"Ha-ha, very funny, Dad," said Kevin. "I'm serious. I heard from one of the other guys that Coach Williams is worried about his job."

"Seriously?" I asked. I liked Coach Williams, even if he did call me "Little Sloan" and even if I wasn't ever going to get to play football for him. He made some bad decisions, but he was a nice person. "That's not fair. He's a good coach, right?"

"He's a great coach!" Kevin snapped, like I was the one threatening his job. "But people want to blame somebody. And it looks like Coach Williams is it unless we can start winning. And, Dad? No one has used the word 'foxy' in, like, fifty years."

—————

We never really planned it, but Jamie and I developed this ritual. On Sunday mornings we would call each other and talk on the phone. The idea was to go over our "venture." (That's what I decided to call it.) We would make sure we had people on each side of the bet and be certain we hadn't forgotten something.

But after we did that, we'd just talk. We'd talk about our weekend. We'd talk about our parents and how they were (or sometimes, amazingly, weren't) driving us crazy. We'd talk about sports. We'd talk about nothing important.

And it was hard not to notice: Every time I hung up, I was in a good mood.

After one of those Sunday talks, when I arrived at my locker on Monday morning, Jamie was there. So were a cluster of other kids, waiting like baby birds to get worms from their mother. And the thing is, I was loving it. In California, I used to kind of slink into school hoping nobody saw me. All I'd be thinking about was getting to a classroom where there would be a teacher nearby. Here, kids called my name when I walked in. Or shouted out my nickname!

"Hey, Rookie Bookie! See you at your locker?" Mark Sterner yelled that morning. "Catch that game, Mitch?" Rudy Matthews asked me. "Some touchdown, huh?" His girlfriend, Rachel Miller, was holding his hand. "We're going to the movies tonight to celebrate," she said, beaming at me. "Thanks, Mitch!"

And there were other kids, saying hi, slapping me high fives. I didn't even know all their names. I didn't care that much. It just felt good. Really good.

Okay, maybe it wasn't exactly like having friends. They didn't invite me over to their houses after school. They didn't crowd around my table to eat with me at lunch. But they didn't trip me, or elbow me, or slam me into the lockers, or stick my head in a toilet either.

I'd take it.

Jamie took out her notebook and crossed off the names as I paid everyone. Or started to pay them.

"Hold on, hold on," I said to Josh Burke. Or I kind of said it to his shirt collar. He was an eighth grader and (like my good pal Carl Lake) he played basketball. And he was tall. Big all over, really.

"Hold on?" he asked. "Hey, Rookie Bookie, I don't want to hold on. I won. Where's my money?"

"I *know* you won. I've *got* your money," I said, irritated. "I just don't have change."

This kept coming up, just like that first day. Most of the kids placed their bets with ten-dollar bills. Sometimes they handed me or Jamie twenties and expected us to have change.

But we had to give each winner eighteen dollars. That meant a ten and a five and three ones. Or three fives and three ones. Whatever, it meant ones. I was always running out of ones.

I didn't want to go back to Irma again. She hadn't looked too happy about making change for me. And that had been when I only needed about eighty dollars' worth. Business had expanded since then. I was actually carrying around hundreds of dollars now, every Monday morning. Me and Jamie both. (Jamie and I. Sorry, Mom.) Irma was sure to get really suspicious if we asked for that much.

I asked my dad and mom and Kevin sometimes, but they were starting to wonder what I needed so many singles for. Whenever I went into a store, I tried to pay with a twenty and squirrel away the change. But it was never enough. And now I was out of ones. Again.

"Look, I've just got twenties," I said to Josh.

"No problem," he said. And before I could stop him, he reached over and grabbed a twenty-dollar bill from my fist.

"Well, okay." He could at least have waited until I handed it to him. "You've got two bucks?"

"Nope." He was chewing gum, and he kept chewing it and smiling.

"So how are you going to give me my change?"

"Sorry, Rookie Bookie. I'm just like you. I don't have change." Josh grinned and chewed and started walking back down the hall.

I was stunned. At least he was our last customer that day, so nobody else got the bright idea of stealing from us. But—*hey!*

Jamie had her hand on my arm.

"Better let him go, Mitch," she said quietly.

"But he—he can't do that! That's our money! He stole our money!"

"So what are we going to do about it, Mitch? Start a fight? Go to a *teacher?*"

She was right. It shouldn't have surprised me, but it did.

Should we knock on the door of the principal's office? *Oh, Mr. Pearlman, Josh Burke just stole two dollars from our gambling business.*

What gambling business, Mr. Sloan? Ms. Spielberger?

Right. Time to cut your losses, Mitch.

"Just forget it," Jamie said, stuffing her money into her backpack. "But we've got to come up with a better way of making change!"

———

That Friday, Jonasburg played a game on the road. The opponent was Gas City, a town name that had made me laugh all week. I told Jamie that I figured that the motto was something like "Excuse me, I don't know what I ate."

"Actually, I think it's 'It wasn't me; it was the dog,'" she said. "Or maybe 'Pull my finger.'"

Besides us, no one else laughed much. I guess they'd all heard this for years and just took it for granted. Besides, Gas City had a lousy team, and everyone was more concerned with the idea that Jonasburg might win a game, which they hadn't done yet this season.

Mom, Dad, and I got into the car to drive to Gas City for the game. Right after we pulled onto the highway, the car started making this funky noise, like there was a squirrel in the engine compartment, trying to get out.

"Oh no," Dad groaned. "I'm going to have to call Walter again."

It's never a good sign when you're on first-name terms with your mechanic. "Didn't Walter just fix something last month? The fuel pump or whatever?" I asked.

"Yes, Mitch," Mom said.

I knew that tone in her voice. That *Mitch is being annoying* tone. But there was still something I wanted to know.

"Why don't you trade this car in, then?" I asked. "If you're always fixing it up. That costs a lot of money."

"Of course it does, Mitch," Dad said. "But we've paid for this car already. We've got to keep it running."

"But—"

"Not now, Mitch. Okay?"

It was crazy. Just like Ben Barnes and his Tater Tots. If you bought something, you had to keep it. Or eat it. Even if you didn't like it. Even if it was actually costing you *more* money. It made no sense at all, but nobody wanted to hear it from me.

"Maybe there's free gas in Gas City," I said, trying to lighten the mood. "Or at least discount gas."

"I doubt it," Mom said, either not getting my joke or choosing to ignore it.

I could have bought the gas. By now, I had a thousand dollars in my desk drawer since Jamie and I were offering bets on almost every game. But how was I supposed to explain to my parents where I'd gotten that much money?

Even though I was just taking a few bets, I still couldn't see myself explaining it to them. Or my new nickname at school.

CHAPTER 8

FOLLOWING THE HERD

We didn't say much else as we drove to Gas City. The road threaded its way through small towns, past silos and farms and cornfields. The land was as flat as a game board, so different from the hills of San Francisco, where you could ride your bike just one block and your legs would cry out in pain.

The road we took had just one single lane in each direction. At one point, we got stuck behind a trailer carrying a horse. When I told Dad to try to pass, he told me to "be patient and enjoy the ride." But patience has never been one of my strengths. A few minutes later, I told Dad to honk the horn and motion for the driver of the truck to move over. He turned to me and said, "Are you crazy? That could scare the horse."

The road finally widened when we pulled into Gas City. At the first stoplight, a truck pulled up next to us. The guy in the passenger seat had a thick beard and no neck, at least that I could see. When he grinned, he showed off a gap between his teeth big enough to fit a pencil. It looked like he was trying to say something to us. So, friendly guy that he is, Dad rolled down his window.

"I see y'all are from Jonasburg," the man said slowly.

Uh-oh. One of our first weeks in Jonasburg, I suggested to Mom and Dad that it might help business to put some bumper stickers on the car. It would let people know that, even if we were new in town, we supported the community and were part of the same group.

People love to be part of a group. Doesn't matter if you go to the same church, live in the same neighborhood, or root for the same team—the point is doing it together. So the bumper stickers were supposed to show that Mom and Dad were a part of Jonasburg—and, hey, their art gallery was, too.

I didn't think about how that would play out anytime we left town, especially on the night of a big game when we weren't the home team.

"Right on, we're from Jonasburg!" Dad said proudly.

"Hey, I like your costume," the guy in the truck said, and the other guys in his truck started laughing.

"Sorry, friend," Dad said. "I didn't quite catch that."

"I said that I like your costume, being a hippie for Halloween and all." Again, the guys in the truck laughed. "Trick or treat, hippie!" Mom looked in the rearview mirror, probably trying to see whether I was scared.

Maybe some dads would respond to that by yelling something they're not supposed to yell in front of their kids, or even getting in a fight. I mean, a guy pulls up next to you and insults you? For no good reason? In front of your wife and kid?

Dad saw it differently. He made a V sign with two fingers. "Peace, my brothers."

The light turned green, and the truck blew past us, kicking up some dust, as the passenger leaned out and yelled "Hippie!" right after something that sounded like a nasty curse word.

"What a bunch of obnoxious jerks," Mom said.

"Oh, don't sweat it," Dad said. "Just some guys from a small town out on a Friday night. Let 'em have some fun."

I'm sure those jerks had more fun than we did once they got to the game. It was the same old story for Jonasburg. The way the players handled the ball, you would have thought it had been covered in oil. There were dropped passes and fumbles and snaps to the quarterback that squirted away.

On one play, the Gas City quarterback threw a pass that looked like it was aimed right at Nathan Isaac. It was a sure interception, a chance to redeem himself for running the wrong way in the previous game. Except that the ball collided violently with his hands and hit the ground. The way he gripped his helmet reminded me of Homer Simpson saying

"D'oh!" after putting a knife in a toaster or eating a piece of charcoal. I guess that, on the bright side, by dropping the football, at least Nathan spared himself the embarrassment of running in the wrong direction.

Still, late in the fourth quarter, the game wasn't totally out of reach. Gas City was leading 20–7 when Kevin caught a pass and shuffled past the defense to score his third touchdown of the season. That made the score 20–13. In the bleachers, my parents gave each other a high five in that clumsy way adults do it.

Coach Williams then decided to go for a two-point conversion, rather than kick an extra point. This didn't make much sense to me, but he called the exact same play as before, Kevin caught the pass again, and it was 20–15. Sitting next to me, Mom and Dad beamed, and other parents patted them on their backs.

After the Jonasburg defense did its part, the offense got the ball back again with two minutes to play and a chance to score one more touchdown and win the game. Following a couple of running plays, Coach Williams called his favorite: "Hoosier 23."

Neil Butwipe would take two steps back, pretend to hand the ball off to A.J. Kumar, and hide the ball behind his hip. As the defense tried to tackle A.J., Neil would throw the ball across the field to Kevin.

It worked perfectly. The Gas City players ganged up on A.J.—only to realize that he didn't have the ball. Meanwhile, Neil threw a perfect pass to Kevin, who caught the ball as if it were drawn magnetically to his hands. He did a fancy dance step to free himself from the defender covering him and then started outrunning the Gas City players toward the end zone, widening his lead every ten yards. In the bleachers, the Gas City fans were all booing and yelling something about a penalty and *were the refs blind?* But the Jonasburg fans and parents were cheering louder than they had cheered all year. "Forty, thirty, twenty, ten, TOUCHDOWN!"

A few weeks before, when we played a touch football game in the street after school, I scored a touchdown and did a funny dance. (I thought it was funny, anyway.) Kevin got upset and told me not to be a show-off.

"Act like you've been there, Mitch," he said. "Act like you've been there before."

"Been where?" I said.

"The end zone," he snapped.

I knew what he meant. But Kevin didn't realize that, for some of us, scoring a touchdown isn't something that happens every day. "What if I *haven't* been there before?" I asked him.

"Act like it anyway," he said.

But now, as he scored and his teammates followed him down the field to congratulate him, Kevin forgot all about his modesty. He put the ball on his waist and rotated his hips, like he was hula-hooping or something.

On the sidelines, the coaches were high-fiving each other. Cheerleaders were hugging, and, I could swear, one was wiping tears that were racing down her cheek. Parents behind my parents were hugging. The curse? It was over. Everyone had just gotten immunized from the losing sickness, as Kevin called it.

Except that when I looked at the field, I noticed that the Gas City section was cheering, too. And their coaches were also high-fiving. And their cheerleaders were hugging, too.

Uh-oh.

And then I saw something else. A yellow eyesore. It was like a huge zit on your face. Like an ugly stain on a beautiful painting. It was a penalty flag that one of the officials had thrown down on the grass.

Pretty soon, everyone else on the Jonasburg side noticed it, too. Three officials came together in the middle of the field, looking like grazing zebras standing in the grass with all their black-and-white stripes. They had a short conversation, and one guy broke away from the others. Facing the Gas City side of the field, he pointed to Jonasburg and gave the signal for holding. Kevin's touchdown wouldn't count.

The Gas City side cheered and whooped. So did their players. Our players slammed their helmets to the ground in frustration. In our bleachers, people said things I can't repeat.

"Boooooo! Hissssssss!" someone nearby yelled angrily. I looked over and it was . . . Dad?

On the one hand, I should have known. No one else would say "hiss." On the other hand, Dad was the guy who got called a hippie by a bunch of bullies earlier in the evening and let it glide off his back. Now he was red-faced with anger over a referee's call? He caught my eye and knew what I was thinking.

"What?" he said. "Those refs are a bunch of cheaters!"

In my new, non-annoying state, I knew that it wasn't the right time to mention this. But the officials probably weren't cheating. They were just acting like...well, like normal people act.

Like I said before, we all want to be part of a group. Let's say you take a test and one of the questions is "What is the capital of Michigan?" You write "Lansing," and you're pretty sure you're right. But after the test, the first eight people you talk to all wrote "Detroit." So now you're probably second-guessing yourself, right?

Now imagine you have to yell out the answer, quick, instead of writing it down. Eight people are yelling "Detroit!" right in your ear. Even if you think they have it wrong, you might go with their answer.

Now pretend you're that referee in the football game at Gas City. You have to make a split-second decision. The home crowd is screaming at you to make that decision one way. (Hardly anyone on the opposing side is screaming at you to make it the other way.) It's easy to see how you could listen to the crowd and do what they want. And, don't forget, these refs probably live in Gas City and have to deal with the people in the crowd the next day after the game.

This is why home teams get a lot more favorable calls—whether it's pitches in baseball, fouls in basketball, or penalties in football.

Not that this was the time to explain this to Dad.

"I didn't know you cared about sports so much," I said.

"We don't, Mitch," Mom said. "But we care about justice and treating people fairly."

And she patted my dad on the arm and got him to sit down and look a little less crazy.

That Sunday, Jamie didn't just want to check in over the phone. She wanted me to come over. So we sat in her backyard, throwing a slobbery tennis ball for her golden retriever, Pepper.

"Mitch," she said quietly, "I've been thinking. Maybe we shouldn't be doing the betting thing anymore."

"What?"

I turned to stare at her. "Why? It's going great. How much money have you made?"

"You know how much, Mitch."

"About two hundred and fifty dollars," I said proudly.

Pepper came galloping back with the drooly ball in her mouth. Jamie continued, "I don't know. I think we're going to get into trouble if we keep it up."

"It's not against the rules."

"Come on, Mitch. If it's not against the rules, why didn't you go to Mr. Pearlman on Monday when Josh walked off with our two dollars?"

"Okay, then." I wrestled the ball out of Pepper's mouth. "So maybe Mr. Pearlman wouldn't like it that much if he found out. But it's not like we're doing something *wrong*. Are we?"

She shrugged.

"We're not making anybody bet. We're not cheating. We're not stealing money like Josh Burke!"

"Yeah, Mitch, I know. But even so. It's almost not fair. Look."

She took out her notebook, folded back a few pages, and showed me a chart that she had made.

week	$Bet	$Won
1	$10	$18
2	$10	—
3	$10	$18
4	$10	—
5	$10	$18
6	$10	—
7	$10	$18
8	$10	—
9	$10	$18
Total	$90	$90

"What are you showing me?" I asked. "What am I supposed to notice?"

"Look at it closely," she said. "You're always so impatient!"

I looked again. She must have seen that I still didn't get the point that she was trying to make.

"So this person bets ten dollars for nine weeks. They won five times in nine weeks. And they only broke even. Look here, they put in ninety dollars and they got back ninety dollars."

"So what?" I asked.

"So, they won five out of the nine games—that's more than fifty-five percent, more than half. That's pretty good. And they only broke even."

"So?"

"So..." Now *she* was the one getting impatient. "Let's say we each put in five bucks and flip a coin nine times, splitting the total ten dollars based on how many times each of us wins. You win five times, more than half of the flips. I only win four. But you still only get your five dollars back."

Ah-ha. Now I got her point.

And I had a comeback.

"But that's the thing!" I said. "Flipping a coin is random. It's a fifty-fifty chance, heads versus tails.

So I would insist on fifty-fifty odds. This is different. I probably think I know more about football than you do, that I have a special skill, that I'm going to be right. So I'll settle for less than fifty-fifty odds."

"Yeah," she said, "but imagine you took a test and got more than half of it right and still ended up with no credit. You might as well not have taken the test at all!"

"Okay," I said, "but they have fun betting on their teams. Much more fun than taking a test, right? It isn't just about winning."

"It just doesn't feel right, Mitch." She sighed and flipped the notebook shut, then turned to her dog. "Look, Pepper, you have to drop the ball if you want me to throw it again." The big shaggy dog loved fetching that slimy ball, but she hated giving it away.

"Listen, Jamie." I was starting to feel weird about this. Panicky, even. I didn't want to quit running the business. And I didn't want Jamie to quit either. "Anybody could figure that out, right? What you just did with your notebook?"

"Sure, but I don't think anybody has."

"That's not our fault, right?"

"Yeah, but—"

I didn't let her finish. "And we don't *know* it's against the rules. Right? Nobody ever said. So you can't quit now! Please. We have to keep it going."

"Why, Mitch?" She turned to me, looking a little worried. "What's the big deal? Why can't we stop now, before anything goes wrong?"

It was a good question. What *was* the big deal? Why *couldn't* we just quit?

I looked away from her, across her yard. It was a nice yard. A big deck. Chrysanthemums in pots. Maple trees starting to turn yellow and orange.

Pepper whined eagerly around the tennis ball in her mouth.

"I never told you why we really left California," I said.

CHAPTER 9

UNDERWATER

We didn't just move to Indiana because we wanted to. My folks got in "turbulent financial water," as I overheard a banker once put it to my dad.

Mom and Dad had never made a lot of money. Some days they would sell a painting or a piece of pottery. But most days they sold nothing at all.

That was okay. We were never rich. Or even close to rich. We were as far from Warren Buffett as Mercury is from Pluto. But we had enough money to live on.

I know, because I used to help keep track of it.

"Mitch, since you like money so much, why don't you help us make a family budget?" Dad once asked me.

I figured out how much we earned as a family and how much we spent, everything from house payments to car payments to the allowance Kevin and I got. "How come he gets more money than I do?" I asked.

"He's older," Mom said.

So unfair.

Anyway, I told Mom and Dad that as long as nothing unexpected happened, we were fine and should even be able to save a few hundred dollars a month.

But last year something unexpected *did* happen. A lot of people started to struggle with their money. They had less of it. People lost their jobs, or their investments weren't doing so well. Companies were making less money, too.

When people are worried about their money, they save it for things they really need, like food and gas. They don't spend it on art. And when people stopped buying art, then it was my parents who started to struggle.

Entire weeks went by without Mom selling a painting or Dad selling any crafts. "Maybe you need to advertise more," I suggested. But they didn't.

"Advertising costs money, Mitch." Dad sighed.

Pretty soon they weren't able to pay the rent on their shop and started selling their things out of our home. Which was fine when we *had* a home.

"I don't think you made the payment on the house this month," I told Dad. "You owe the bank money."

"We don't have it, Mitch," he said matter-of-factly.

Oh no.

Eventually this guy from the bank came by the house, a short, plump man with a mustache that looked like a caterpillar on his upper lip and a short-sleeve dress shirt with stains under the armpits, just like Coach Williams's. (Except that Coach Williams was running around on a football field, not sitting in our living room.) The man told us the bank might be "foreclosing" on our house at 353 Del Rio Avenue.

"What's that mean?" Kevin asked me.

"It means that the bank gave Mom and Dad a loan to pay for the house. And Mom and Dad have to pay back the bank," I said. "And since they can't pay back the money, the bank is going to want the house back."

"What's a bank want with our house?"

It was a good question. Does a bank really want a three-bedroom home with bike tire tracks on the walls, a gaping hole in the ceiling from where Kevin once swung on a ceiling fan (don't ask how it happened), and a skateboard ramp in the back?

But I guess, from the bank's point of view, getting our house was better than not getting anything.

That's when we ran into another problem.

The price of the house had gone down. Not just our house, actually. House prices all over California—all over the country—were way down. So our house was worth less than it was when

Mom and Dad bought it. Even if we sold the house, we wouldn't have enough money to pay the bank back (and we wouldn't have a place to live).

So they did what a lot of people did. They decided to hand the house over to the bank and start fresh somewhere else. It was sort of like a do-over in a game of kickball.

As always, I tried to explain it to Kevin in a way he could understand. "Let's say you wanted to buy a vintage baseball card of Willie Mays, the all-time greatest San Francisco Giant—"

"I could never afford that," he interrupted. "That would cost, like, thousands of dollars!"

"That's okay," I said. "A bank would buy it for you. You just have to promise to pay them back the money—plus a little more in interest."

"That's ridiculous," he said. "How could I pay it back? I can't even save my allowance each week."

"But the bank thinks you can pay them back eventually. And maybe even by the time you want to sell the card, it could be worth at least the same amount as what you bought it for, maybe even more, and you would have already paid them most of the money."

Kevin started smiling. I'm sure he was picturing himself showing the card off to his friends and framing it for his wall. I had to cut off his daydreaming.

"There's only one problem," I said. "What if the value of the card went down? Let's say you paid three thousand dollars for the card, and then suddenly you owed the bank three thousand dollars plus interest for a baseball card that at the most you could only sell for, like, one thousand dollars? Even if you sold the card, you'd still owe the bank more than two grand, and they want it back!"

His smile went to half-mast. Then it collapsed entirely.

"I'd be in trouble," he said. "I'd probably just have to give the card back to the bank or whatever."

"Exactly."

So that's what my mom and dad did. Ditched the house. Gave it back to the bank. Moved out here to Indiana to start over.

And it wasn't so bad. I sure didn't miss school

back in California. Kevin was playing football (and losing, but at least he had fun being good at it). I was making friends, and maybe even a *best* friend.

So I told all this to Jamie, and she listened, petting Pepper, looking serious and thinking.

"Okay, I get it," she said. "That sounds rough. I'm sorry, Mitch. But what does it have to do with the betting at school?"

I sighed. "They're not selling a lot of art here either," I told her. "I didn't mind it, moving once. But I really don't want to have to do it again. I like it here. People like *me* here."

"So you want to keep making money at school? Just in case?"

I nodded.

"Okay, then. We will."

Suddenly Jamie was all business. "I know what to do about the change thing, Mitch. This'll work."

And she told me her plan. We'd give the kids who placed their bets using one-dollar bills first choice of the games. Kids who wanted to pay with tens and twenties could bet, too—but only *after* the ones who paid with singles.

Genius.

And Jamie had another great idea. Right after we'd paid off the winners, we'd show them the schedule of the next weekend's games and give them the chance to put down their bets. It worked great. As long as they had the money handy—and were feeling good about how talented they were at predicting football games—why not let them make more bets?

They did, too. They were *glad* to do it.

The money kept piling up in my dresser drawer.

And Jamie didn't talk about quitting anymore.

———

Remember how I said that my day would usually peak with math? Well, that wasn't the case lately.

It seemed like Mr. Rafferty was starting to... well...I don't want to say he had it in for me, but I could tell that he didn't like me as much as he used to. He didn't call on me a lot—sometimes even when I was the only one with a hand in the air. He never laughed at the jokes I made.

And please don't bother trying to suggest that

it was "in my head" or that I was "imagining it." That's the kind of thing grown-ups say. And I know it's not true.

Mr. R. was teaching us about integers—positive and negative numbers. And as usual, he had come up with a fun way to do it: a fake game show. He called it *Mathletes in Action*.

When it was my turn to be the featured contestant, Mr. R. stared me right in the eye and spoke extra slowly. "Okay, sir," he said in a fake game-show-host voice. "For the benefit of the folks watching at home all around this great nation, please state your name and your affiliation."

"Mitch Sloan. Jonasburg Middle School."

"Very good. With everyone at Jonasburg Middle School cheering you on, Mitch Sloan, are you ready for your first question?"

I don't know how Mr. Rafferty always had the energy to be so lively and funny. Especially compared to Mrs. Connor, my social studies teacher, who once showed us a movie and fell asleep in the middle of it. Or Mrs. Shelby, my fifth-grade teacher, who would sometimes try to sneak out her phone, place it in her lap, and send text messages to her friends while we were filling out the worksheets she assigned. But Mr. R.? He's like those athletes who "always bring their A game," like the announcers say.

Listening to his introduction, I almost started to crack up, but I held it together. "Yes, sir," I said. "I'm ready."

"Okay," he said, staying in character. "Everyone at your school is suddenly interested in gambling on professional football games."

Did I hear that right? Did he really just—

"This is cleeeeearly against school rules. Kids? Gambling on football? That's not right. But your usual good judgment eluuuuudes you, Mitch. And you do it anyway."

I did hear it right.

My classmates were starting to laugh.

"Here's the question, Mitch Sloan: You bet ten dollars one week and win eighteen when your team proves victorrrrious."

Wait, he even knows the amounts? How is that possible?

"The second week, you waaaaager ten dollars

and lose the bet. The question: What integer represents your total winnings?"

I stood frozen like one of those lawn gnomes. Except that lawn gnomes don't blush from a combination of shame and embarrassment.

"I'll repeat the question: What integer represents your winnings from gaaaambling?"

Oh, that word again. I may as well give him the right answer.

"Minus two," I finally whispered, my heart beating faster than ever.

"Yes! You wagered twenty dollars and made eighteen. So your winnings come to an integer of minus two! Which means you actually *lost* two dollars. Thanks for playing, Mitch. You have made your classmates—and yourself—so, so proud."

For the first time in Mr. R.'s math class, the bell couldn't ring soon enough.

━━━

From there, my day somehow got worse. Of course it did. It's like a rule of middle school. If something goes wrong in the morning, you can bet that something else will go wrong in the afternoon. Every now and then, you get a day when you should have stayed in bed. And this was one of those days.

I walked into fifth-period science class, where Mrs. Wolff always collects the homework right after the bell rings. I reached into my folder to pull out a worksheet she'd assigned about continental drift. I always keep my homework in the pocket on the left side. But when I looked, it was empty. *Hmmm. That's strange.*

I opened my science textbook, thinking maybe I had folded the worksheet in half and left it in the book. But when I fanned out the pages, nothing fell out. Maybe it was in my locker. But I couldn't go back to check without a hall pass. And Mrs. Wolff wasn't going to give me one of those—at least not until after the homework was collected.

I got that awful panicky feeling. You know, when your mouth goes dry, like all the saliva has been drained. When your stomach feels like it's doing a gymnastics routine. And then your palms get all the moisture that's missing from your mouth.

As I started flipping through my science folder one last, desperate time, I felt a tap on my shoulder. I turned around and it was Clint Grayson, flashing a smile that revealed teeth the color of creamed corn. When his lips turned up, I could see the beginning of the mustache he was growing.

"Looking for this?" he said in his goofy voice, holding up my homework.

"Give it to me!" I said, feeling the anger start to flare up.

"I would," he said, "except for one little thing."

"What's that?"

"I don't really want to," he snarled.

"Give. Me. My. Homework," I said again. Panic was totally giving way to rage.

"Do you want to try and make me?" he asked.

This felt like a dance I hadn't done in a while. The Bully Dance. And the step-by-step choreography was coming back to me.

You know what I hate the most about bullies? It's not just that they humiliate you. It's that they turn everyone else against you, too. As Clint teased me, I looked back and saw that Mark Sterner was laughing, along with a lot of other kids. Rudy Matthews was grinning and Rachel Miller was snickering with a hand over her mouth.

I didn't even care about the homework. This is going to sound arrogant, and probably annoying, too, but I knew I was going to get a good final grade in science, even if I got a zero on this particular assignment.

I cared more that Clint was embarrassing me in front of other kids. Mark and Rudy and Rachel? All of them were part of the betting pool. Mark was in my fantasy football league. Rudy and I had played H-O-R-S-E during recess just last week. Why were they siding with Clint? It's like they wanted to be on the side of the person with more power, even if he was mean and wrong and acting like a jerk.

I wasn't going to overpower Clint and get my homework back. I knew that, and so did he. So I tried to act like a businessman and treat this as a negotiation.

"Okay," I said, rolling my eyes. "What do I have to do to get my homework back?"

He had his answer ready. "Give me one of them football bets for free."

No way. That was a deal breaker, as they say in business.

1) Jamie and I had agreed that we wouldn't make any decisions without first talking to each other.
2) If I did that for Clint, every kid who wanted a free bet would just steal my homework and hold it for ransom. I'd be vulnerable. And Jamie might be, too.
3) It was just flat-out wrong. I wasn't going to let this jerk get what he wanted, just because he was bigger than I was, and a star on the football team, and he had my home-work assignment in his disgusting hands.
4) A basic business rule: If you give some-thing away for free, it's not worth as much anymore.

"No deal," I said.

"Okay, then. Have it your way." He tossed the

paper back at me. Of course it drifted to the floor and I had to lean down to grab it.

I couldn't believe Clint Grayson had given my homework back so easily. I'd said no to him, and he hadn't even cared? What was up with that? Bullies never let you get away with "no." They always find a way to make you pay.

Clint saw that I was confused.

"Don't need one little piece of homework," he said, grinning. "I've got something a lot better. Should have given me my free bet, little Mitch. You're gonna be sorry about that."

I turned my back on him and sat down, like I didn't care. But it was an act. If he was trying to make me nervous, it was working.

CHAPTER 10

BE RICH OR BE HAPPY?

School let out at 3:15, but that still left plenty of time for the day to get even worse. Which it did. When I got off the bus and walked to our front door, I got that panicky feeling for the second time. I couldn't find my house keys.

That used to happen to me all the time in California. This was the first time it had happened since we moved. With all the distractions of the day—the one hundred and twenty dollars in cash that I was carrying in my pockets; Mr. R. making it clear that he knew about the football pool; Clint Grayson and his rotting teeth, not to mention his threats—I'd forgotten to take my keys off the peg in my locker.

Even though it would mean risking a lecture filled with words like "responsibility" and "accountability," I grabbed my bike and headed to Mom and Dad's store to borrow their keys.

When I got there, Dad was sitting on his stool, legs crossed, playing his guitar. I recognized the first chords of "Sweet Home Alabama." Not a customer in sight.

"Hey, Mitch," he said. "How's tricks?"

"What tricks?" I asked.

"How's tricks?" he said slowly. "The kids don't say that one anymore?"

"Maybe not so much," I said. *Add it to the list*. . . . "Where's Mom?"

"In the studio, working on a new painting," he said, readjusting his ponytail. "Though I'm not sure what for."

"What do you mean?"

"I think we underestimated Indiana as an art

market," Dad said, chuckling. "Not a lot of demand, you might say. That sounds like one of those business phrases you use, Mitch."

"Are you worried?"

"No," Dad replied. "Not at all." But I could tell he was.

Now my lousy day at school seemed almost silly. This was serious. Without thinking it through, I reached into my pockets and pulled out five of the six twenty-dollar bills I had stuffed in there.

"That reminds me," I said, unfurling the money. "There's a kid in my grade whose mom wanted to buy a painting from you. One that costs a hundred dollars."

"Really?" Dad said. "You're not pulling my leg?"

"No, I have the money right here," I said. "It was a watercolor...."

"A hundred-dollar watercolor? Hmmm. Oh, it must be the small one of the covered bridge," Dad said, suddenly excited.

"Yeah, that's the one," I lied.

"But why didn't your friend's mom just come by herself?"

"Um, uh, I think that she was too busy with work," I lied again.

"Well, that's too bad. I would have liked to explain the details to her," Dad said. "Mom worked hard on getting the shade of red just right."

He started to wrap up the painting but then stopped. "Do you know the woman's name? I'd like to write her a thank-you note and let her know that she can exchange the painting if it's not the one she had in mind. I'll put her on the mailing list, too."

"Uh, no," I said.

"What's your friend's last name?" he said. "I can look up their address and drop it off on the way home from work."

"I forget," I said, less than smoothly. "I'll just take it."

Fortunately, Dad doesn't really do suspicion. He's too trusting, too look-on-the-bright-side, and too all-around nice of a guy for that. Besides, he didn't figure I could have possibly had a hundred dollars on my own. "Well, I guess if she gave you a hundred dollars, she must really want it!"

"Exactly."

"Your mom loved that painting," Dad said. "This sure will make her happy!"

And me, too. I was out a hundred dollars, but I still had twenty in my pocket and a bunch more at home. I had done a good thing for Mom and Dad. (Plus, I was now the proud owner of a painting of a covered bridge.) Once Dad applied the last layer of Bubble Wrap, I stuck the package into my backpack and rode off.

———

On the way home, I realized that, with all my panicked lying, I had completely forgotten to get the keys, which was the reason I went to the store in the first place. Now I had some time to kill, so I took a detour past Jamie's house. She was sitting on her front steps typing on a laptop when I rode up. "Hey, Mitch!" she shouted.

"Oh, hey," I said from my bike. "Hey, Jamie."

"What are you doing around here?" she asked.

"Just out for a bike ride," I said. Another lie. They were really starting to pile up.

Bending the truth for Dad by pretending that the mom of a mystery classmate wanted to spend a hundred bucks on a painting? I could get away with that. Bending the truth for Jamie? That was tougher.

"Yeah, right." She smirked. "If you wanted to hang out, you should have just asked. Wait a sec for me to put my dad's laptop back in the house. I'll get my bike, too."

We rode around the neighborhood. Since there weren't many cars, we mostly pedaled side by side. I was going to tell her about Clint Grayson stealing my homework in science, but she'd already heard about it.

"You should have told him to put his name on it and hand it in as his own," she said. "It would have been the only time in his life he could've experienced the feeling of seeing an A on the top of the page."

That made me feel better. "Before that, in Mr. R.'s class, he pretended to be a game show host," I went on. "When it was my turn to be the contestant, my problem was all about a football gambling pool."

"Probably just a coincidence," she said nonchalantly.

"A betting pool where you put down ten dollars for the chance to win eighteen?"

"Oh," said Jamie. "A coincidence. Ish."

"And then to top it all off, I left the keys to my house in my locker," I said.

"So, not such a good day, huh?"

"No," I agreed. "Not really."

"It'll get better," she promised. "I mean, things do, right? You go through these crappy days and nothing goes right and you think, okay, this is my life, this is what it's always going to be like. And the next day it's all back to normal. Hey, I lost something, too, today. My notebook. That's why I was working on Dad's laptop when you accidentally-on-purpose came by."

I let that crack go. But, wait—

"You lost the notebook?" I said, skidding to a stop. Jamie sailed on ahead. "With all our information in it, who bet on what teams and how much?"

She stopped her bike and turned back to me.

"It'll turn up," she said. "I'm not worried. Come on, Mitch, ride."

She wasn't worried? That made one of us.

When we got to the Meadowbrook Park apartment complex, we stopped riding and sat on a picnic table.

"Let me ask you something, Mitch," she said. "What are you doing with all your money?"

I couldn't tell her how I'd bought a painting to help my parents' lame business out. That was kind of embarrassing. Plus, I didn't want her to catch me in another lie. "Nothing, really," I said. "It's mostly in my room. Why?"

"Why? Because we've each made three hundred and fifty dollars already. That's a lot of allowance. And I haven't really spent much of it either. That's kind of weird, isn't it?"

"I don't know," I said. "I think that *having* money makes me happy. And if I spent it, I wouldn't have it."

"So are you?"

"Am I what?" I asked.

"Happy," Jamie said. "Are you glad to have three hundred and fifty dollars you didn't have just a few weeks ago?"

Actually, in my case it was two hundred and fifty. But I didn't tell her that. "I guess," I said. "I mean, yeah. It makes me feel better, having that money around. In case...you know." She nodded, remembering what I'd told her about my parents.

"But really," I went on, "it just feels good to have an idea no else had. It felt good to have a plan and then put it into action. It felt good that my actions turned into a profit."

Plus, it felt good to be liked by a bunch of other kids. Or sort-of-liked. Being the Rookie Bookie was better than being "Mitch with a swirly." And it felt best of all to have Jamie as a business partner.

But was I actually *happier* being rich? I hadn't thought about it before, but—no. Not exactly. I was still me, still Mitch. Not that much had changed because of the cash stuffed into the back of my dresser drawer.

Our conversation was interrupted when we both looked up at the sky. It had turned from gray into something uglier, almost the color of a bruise.

"Just a Midwestern fall storm, California boy," Jamie said.

"Is it coming or going?" I asked.

"Coming," she said. "It's definitely coming."

CHAPTER 11

THE PRISONER'S DILEMMA

Then, on Monday, like someone flipped a switch, everything came to an end. My smooth adjustment to a new town and a new school. My booming business. Pretty much my life as I knew it.

I was sitting in math class, learning about irrational numbers, when static crackled over the loudspeaker. The voice of Ms. Minton, the office administrator, blasted through the air. "Mitch Sloan, please report to the assistant principal's office. I repeat: Would Mitch Sloan please report to

Assistant Principal Allegra's office?" She phrased it like a question, but it was really a command.

I'm going to let you in on a little secret. If you're worried about getting sent to the principal's office, well, forget it. The person you *really* have to fear is the assistant principal. Principals are like CEOs of big companies, captains of big ships, generals of big armies. They're in charge of the whole enterprise, and they spend most of their time in boring meetings, dealing with Big Issues. They deal with parents, with the superintendent, with the newspapers, and so on. They don't usually deal with the students.

The assistant principals? They're the eyes and ears of their schools, the ones who really know what's going on. They're the ones you have to watch out for.

Without saying a word—in fact, without even looking me in the eye—Mr. Rafferty scribbled out a hall pass and put it in my hand. He looked disappointed. Like he had asked me for a favor that I forgot to do. I made the long walk down to the office. My guess was that Mrs. Allegra was not calling me because she wanted to offer a belated welcome to the new kid, or to tell me that I had won Student-of-the-Week honors. I had a sinking feeling this was about one thing and one thing only.

I tried to put the negative thoughts out of my head, and I walked into the office wearing my brightest, blue-ribbon smile, a trick I learned from one of those business books. People don't want to make deals with somebody who looks miserable or angry. Looking cheerful and confident is the way to go.

The smile quickly melted away when I saw Mrs. Allegra. She was sitting behind her desk, glasses riding low on her nose. She was peering down at some sort of report, looking as though she had just smelled an overflowing toilet.

I could see a framed picture next to her computer. She was posed with two boys who looked about Kevin's age—her sons, I guessed—in front of the Saint Louis Arch. Everyone was wearing shorts and sunglasses. It was probably a family trip over the summer. Mrs. Allegra looked a lot happier in that photo than she did now.

"Hi, I'm Mitch!" I said as cheerfully as I could, extending my arm for a handshake. She didn't look up. This. Was. About. To. Get. Ugly.

Mrs. Allegra didn't waste time. "Do you know why you're here, Mitchell?"

Mitchell? The only person who calls me Mitchell is my grandmother. Not that this was the right time to discuss my preferred name.

"Not really," I lied. I noticed that I had been doing that an awful lot lately.

"Well, it's about the little gambling ring you've been running. Actually, I shouldn't say little. A concerned student handed this notebook in to me yesterday. And if the information on this piece of paper is correct, you took in a thousand dollars in bets for this week alone. One. Thousand. Dollars."

Gambling *ring*? That made it sound so bad. Like it was illegal or something.

When she pulled out the notebook, I recognized it immediately. It was Jamie's. The one she had lost yesterday. Whoever found it must have been surprised to see that, among the poems and stories

151

and journal entries, there were betting records for over thirty football games.

"Don't worry," Mrs. Allegra spit out. "I've already spoken with your co-conspirator."

Co-conspirator? That made it sound even more serious, like illegal drugs or something. And what was Jamie thinking right now? What had she said already? I could feel the panic rising up in my throat. I tried to remain calm.

"Well, it wasn't like we were going to keep the thousand dollars," I explained very reasonably. "We only take a percentage of the—"

"I'm not finished. Do you have any idea how serious this is?"

"I didn't know I was doing anything wrong. I just assumed—"

"Never assume," she snapped, cutting me off again. "This has been a mystery for weeks, and we'd found a lot of clues. Now you're going to help us solve it."

"Clues?" I thought I said this to myself but apparently not.

"Yes, Mitchell. Clues," Mrs. Allegra said, slowing her voice down. "It started a few weeks ago, when a teacher wondered why on Monday mornings there was always a gathering of students in front of your locker. And why they were all wearing guilty looks when he walked by. I believe 'masks of shame' was his exact phrase."

"Well, I can—"

"Does it sound like I'm through? Next, Irma the cafeteria cashier reported that, several weeks ago, you had nervously asked her to make eighty dollars' worth of change in one-dollar bills. We also found this notebook belonging to your friend Jamie Spielberger. In addition to some rather sarcastic comments about the intelligence level of some classmates and the physical appearance of teachers, there was this."

Here, Mrs. Allegra opened Jamie's notebook and flipped through pages and pages filled with notes and charts about football games and money owed and paid.

"And when I called your parents this morning to ask for their help in solving this conundrum, they said that you had paid for a painting of a covered bridge with one hundred dollars in cash. You said it was for a classmate, but then they found the painting under your bed. I think you know you've been up to no good."

I really didn't see what she was getting so upset about. Okay, maybe there was some school rule against gambling I hadn't known about. (*That you didn't want to know about*, my brain whispered. *Never even tried to find out about*.) But really, what was so wrong with helping people out? All the old arguments, the ones I'd used with Jamie, popped back up in my mind. I hadn't lied, hadn't cheated, hadn't stolen anything.

People had wanted to place bets. I'd just helped. I'd helped my parents, too, by buying that painting. What was so wrong?

But then I thought about how angry Mrs. Allegra was, how worried Jamie had been weeks ago, how Mr. Rafferty had looked so disappointed in me. How I had lied to my parents.

"Now, Mitchell, why don't you connect the dots and explain this whole scheme?"

A scheme? A co-conspirator? Evidence? Witnesses? A gambling ring? Mrs. Allegra was making this sound like a real criminal investigation. It occurred to me that, before I said anything else, I should talk with Jamie and make sure we had our stories straight.

As if she had been reading my mind, Mrs. Allegra cut in again with her stern voice. "And don't bother trying to check in with your friend. We've had enough of your machinations."

I had never even heard that word before. But it didn't sound good.

"I don't know who's responsible for what, who's the ringleader, and who was just going along with a bad idea, Mitchell," she said. "But I called Jamie Spielberger down fifteen minutes ago. She's in the office annex and I gave her the same options that I'm about to give you."

Mrs. Allegra then explained my choices. If Jamie and I both kept quiet and didn't reveal exactly what was going on, we would each get a one-day suspension from school, mostly for all the suspicious behavior.

But here was the catch: If one of us confessed the whole plan and the other kept quiet, the person who kept quiet would get six days of suspension and the confessor would get off free for coming clean.

On the other hand, if we *both* confessed, we would each get four days of suspension. Mrs. Allegra sent me to a small empty conference room across from her office and told me I had a few minutes to think about it. When she came back, I would have to give her my answer.

It was kind of confusing, so I sketched out a little chart with boxes of the possibilities, and it looked something like this:

		JAMIE CONFESS	JAMIE KEEP QUIET
MITCH	CONFESS	BOTH GET FOUR DAYS' SUSPENSION.	JAMIE GETS SIX DAYS' SUSPENSION. MITCH GETS NO SUSPENSION.
MITCH	KEEP QUIET	MITCH GETS SIX DAYS' SUSPENSION. JAMIE GETS NO SUSPENSION.	BOTH GET ONE-DAY SUSPENSION.

I thought about what Jamie might do. Would she keep quiet? Or would she tell Mrs. Allegra what had been going on? Jamie wouldn't really rat me out, would she?

Maybe I was thinking about it the wrong way. Looking at my chart, I realized something: It really didn't matter what Jamie did. Whatever she chose, I was better off confessing.

If I thought that Jamie was going to confess, I was better off confessing, too. In that situation, we would each have to do four days of suspension—but that was better than the six days of suspension I would face if I stayed quiet and she didn't.

If she were quiet, I was better off confessing, too. I would be in trouble for zero days—which was better than the one-day suspension if we both kept quiet.

It was pretty tricky of Mrs. Allegra to set us up like that, and I was sure Jamie would figure out that the best thing for both of us to do would be to own up. So I decided to confess everything:

About how I first won a football bet with Jamie. About how that got me thinking and I came up with the idea to run the football pool and talked Jamie into helping me. About how we eliminated all the risk by matching up the ten-dollar bets and not taking one side unless someone else took the other side. About how we collected two bucks on every twenty put into action.

Apparently Jamie confessed, too, because as I told Mrs. Allegra everything I had done wrong, she just looked down at me. Her glasses still riding low on her nose, she looked more bored than surprised. When I finally finished, she shook her head and sighed.

"Well," she said, "you and your pal broke about a dozen school rules—from soliciting on school property to organizing a game of chance. But I will say this: At least you told the truth today. Your story matched with the story of your co-conspirator."

Mrs. Allegra almost sounded nice there for one second. But that quickly changed, and she started in again. "Still, there's no excuse for what you did. No excuse whatsoever. I called your parents to come pick you up. You're welcome to return to school on Monday after spending four days thinking about what I will charitably call an extreme lapse in good judgment."

It was around then that a tall woman wearing black boots and a fur coat stomped into the principal's office area. Jamie's mom.

She looked about the same as she had that time I'd met her at Jamie's house—perfect clothes, perfect hair—except that this time she didn't look at all happy to see me.

When Jamie walked out of the annex, her hair covered most of her face, but I could see that her eyes were rimmed in red. I was surprised that she had been crying. She could skin her arm playing football and not want to leave the game. But I guess everyone has their breaking point.

"Mom," she said.

Mrs. Spielberger was having none of it. "Young lady," she huffed, "I can't even talk to you right now."

"Young lady"? It sounded funny to hear Jamie— a girl who talks more trash than any boy, whose hands are caked in dirt, who chews her fingernails, who burps at volumes that could shatter your eardrums, who can name every quarterback in the league—get called "young lady."

"Hey, Jamie," I said, getting up from my seat and moving toward the doorway of Mrs. Allegra's office.

She turned around and glared at me.

Actually, it was worse than a glare. It was like there were little knives in her eyes and she was trying to stab me. "I wish you had never moved here from California," she said. "You and your stupid get-rich ideas."

Jamie stormed out right after her mother. I felt sick.

Because there was still time for things to get worse, a few minutes later my mom walked in. And where Mrs. Spielberger had looked furious, my mom looked even worse.

Furious I could deal with. My mom looked disappointed, and miserable, and about to cry. I felt awful.

She signed me out of school, and then thanked— *thanked*—Mrs. Allegra.

As we walked out of the office, some of the kids

who had bet in our pool, including Ben and Avni, were waiting outside. Were they in trouble, too? How did Mrs. Allegra know?

Jamie's notebook! We had gotten everyone in trouble. As I brushed past them, I saw them staring intently at me. Not quite as bad as Jamie's glare, but they were mad. Really mad. Then one of the eighth graders shoved me and said, "Heard you made like a thousand dollars off of us. Nice way to treat your friends!"

Except that they weren't really my friends. They had been nice to me because I'd placed bets for them. And now they all hated me *because* I'd placed bets for them. I was less popular than I had ever been in California.

When we finally got outside and into the car, I tried to talk to my mom. I needed someone to understand. "Mom, listen," I started.

"Not now, Mitch," she said quietly. "Really. Not now."

Mom didn't say anything to me on the drive home, which was actually worse than having her yell at me. The expression on her face was more confusion than anything else. Like: *Who are you? This smallish kid wearing the blue hoodie and jeans, with short brown hair and a few freckles on his nose? He looks like my younger son, Mitch. But this kid got suspended for running an illegal gambling ring. That's not the kid we raised. Must be somebody else's. Nope, don't recognize him at all.*

Finally, as we drove past an orchard, Mom ended the patch of silence.

"This is some pretty heavy stuff for a seventh grader," she said with a sigh. "Are you okay?"

"Yeah, I guess." Then it was my turn to sigh. I figured that I may as well tell her the truth, even if it wasn't what she wanted to hear. "In a weird way, I feel kind of relieved. I still don't get why everybody is so mad, though. It wasn't that bad."

"You really don't get it, Mitch?" My mom looked so upset. "You *lied*, for a start. You lied to your teachers and you lied to us. About the bets. About that painting. Couldn't you tell that if you were doing something you had to tell so many lies about, it must be wrong?"

Oh.

Jamie had been worried. Mr. Rafferty had been suspicious. But all along, I'd never felt bad about what I was doing.

I did then, though. Sitting in the car, looking at my mom's face.

"Dad and I really are just so...disappointed, Mitch. You let us down."

And it wasn't just them. I had let Jamie down, too.

CHAPTER 12

AN UNFAIR FIGHT

When we got home, I didn't need to be told to go to my room, and I knew not to go on the computer for any reason, but especially not to play fantasy football. I had a full backpack. Assistant Principal Allegra asked my teachers to put together assignments for the week so I wouldn't fall behind in any classes. But I didn't open any of the books. Mostly I just lay on my bed, tossing a tennis ball in the air and thinking.

Around six, I heard a car pull up, which meant Kevin was home from practice. I looked out my window and saw him unfold himself from the backseat of a sports car. He had changed out of his football uniform, but his hair was matted in sweat and he had streaks of black on his face.

He slammed the car door so hard I could practically feel the house shake, and stormed up the driveway, looking like he wanted to tear somebody apart.

Uh-oh. Could somebody have told him what I did? Was that why he was so mad? It didn't make much sense—but I couldn't think of any other reason for him to look like King Kong on a bad day.

Mom and Dad intercepted Kevin in the driveway. I'm sure they were going to give him advance warning and tell him about his juvenile delinquent brother, if he didn't already know. I ducked down where they wouldn't see me watching them.

Mom and Dad were talking in hushed tones so I couldn't hear very much. But the expression on Kevin's face went from furious to surprised. *What? Are you kidding? Mitch? My kid brother, the one with the spot in the starting lineup of the Honor Roll? He got suspended?*

When Kevin came inside, he walked right to my door and knocked. I opened it up a crack.

"Tough day, huh?" he said.

"You could say that," I muttered. "You, too?"

"Not so much for me." He stood there in my doorway. "But it's true about Coach Williams. He told us today. We've got one more game this season, against our biggest rivals, Clarksville. The Corncob Bowl is the most important game of the year. Both teams agreed to push it back a few weeks just to get ready! If we don't win, he's out of a job."

"Oh." I wandered back over to my bed to flop down on it and stare at the ceiling some more. "That sucks." I couldn't exactly work myself up to feeling all upset; I just didn't have the energy. But I did feel bad for Coach Williams. Even if some of his plays weren't the best, he didn't deserve this.

Kevin sighed. "Hey, at least you didn't get a swirly the way you did in California," he said, watching me. "Remember when you tricked Carl Lake into helping you win that fifty bucks?"

"That's one way to look at it," I said. "On the other hand, I only got wet hair and embarrassment for that. For this football gambling thing, I got suspended."

"'This football gambling thing,'" Kevin said, shaking his head. "I don't want to say I told you so. But I told you so."

"Yeah, you told me." I threw the tennis ball hard enough to bounce sharply off the ceiling, making a loud *thwack*. And I didn't really care when it left a scuff mark.

"Everybody's pretty mad, huh?"

Thwack.

"Yeah."

Thwack.

Kevin shrugged and turned around, headed for the door.

"The thing is, Kevin?" I sat up.

"Yeah?" He turned back around.

"I don't get it. Why everybody's so mad."

"Really?"

I groaned a little. "I'm not trying to be stupid. Okay, I guess I should have checked in about whether gambling at school is against the rules."

"Yeah, that might have been a good idea." Kevin laughed.

"And I *know* it was wrong lying to Mom and Dad. I'm sorry about that. Seriously. But is there really something so terrible about helping people make bets?" I flopped back down on my bed and stared at the ceiling some more. "It's not like I stole from them or lied to them or something."

Kevin came and sat on my bed.

"But you made a lot of money, right?"

"Yeah." *Thwack.* "That's wrong?"

He shook his head. "No, I don't think that's wrong. But the other kids, the ones who were betting? Did they make money?"

"Some of them."

"A lot of them?"

I thought about Jamie's chart, and the way she'd figured out that even if you bet right on half of your games, you still wouldn't break even. "No, probably not."

"So you made a lot of money. And nobody else did."

"So what? That happens all the time in business.

Somebody makes money, somebody doesn't. You don't go to jail if you're the one who makes money. Do you get in trouble if you score more points in a football game than the other team?" *Thwack.*

"No. I don't know, Mitch. But it doesn't feel the same. I guess—it wasn't really a fair fight, the way you did it."

"Not fair?" I felt hot anger bubbling inside of me like lava in a volcano. I threw the ball harder. "I didn't lie. I didn't cheat."

"Yeah, but you kind of—you're really smart, Mitch."

Thwack. "So now I'm in trouble for being smart?"

"No. Shut up. Stop giving me such a hard time. I'm trying to figure it out."

I looked over at Kevin. He really did look like he was thinking hard. So I shut my mouth and let him do it.

Finally he nodded, like something made sense at last. "When I play football, both teams know they're trying to beat the other team," he said. "Right?"

"Right."

"So everybody's playing as hard as they can. Any little advantage you can get, you take it."

"Right."

"But those other kids, the ones who were making the bets? They didn't know it was like a football game to you. They thought they were just fooling around with some of their friends. That it didn't matter how smart they were, and that you were smarter. It was like you were in game mode, and they were in friend mode. You were competing, and they weren't. Maybe that's why everybody got so mad."

Wow.

I was used to explaining money stuff to Kevin. I wasn't used to having him explain something back to me. So I lay there, kind of surprised, thinking about what he'd said. It actually made some sense.

"I don't know, Mitch. But that's what I think, anyway. Hang in there. Nobody stays mad forever." He got up and headed for the door again.

"Kevin?" I said before he got there.

"Yeah?"

"Thanks. But the thing is..." I said quietly, still

staring up at the ceiling, "most of them weren't really my friends, even though I wanted them to be."

He nodded, like he understood what I meant, and then he left.

I lay there, thinking about the one real friend I'd made during this whole year so far, and the look on her face in the assistant principal's office. If anybody in the world could stay mad forever, it might be Jamie Spielberger.

Back in California, a kid in the grade above me was suspended for getting into a fistfight one time. I remember thinking that suspension sounded more like a vacation than a punishment. You have to stay home from school for a few days? Not much difference between that and a weekend.

Wrong.

Mom and Dad made me swear I wouldn't watch television, turn on the computer, play video games, or watch a screen of any kind. Instead, I had to work on all the assignments from school that I was missing. On top of that, they gave me extra assignments to keep me busy. Dad printed out a list of world capitals and told me that I was expected to have them memorized by the time he returned home from work. From Afghanistan (Kabul) to Zimbabwe (Harare).

Mom had given me a list of vocabulary words to commit to memory.

- Illicit: illegal
- Clandestine: held in secret
- Deceiving: tricking or giving a false impression

(Jeez, I wondered whether *all* the words Mom chose were intended to be about my "crime." I was relieved that the rest weren't about me. I think.)

- Corpulent: fat
- Xenophobic: fearful of foreigners
- Diffident: shy
- Craven: cowardly
- Interminable: never-ending

They'd also decided that I was going to have to "make amends" to the Jonasburg school community. "People will feel better about you, and you'll feel better about yourself," Mom said. They were going to call Mrs. Allegra and talk about some ideas for what I could do.

Oh, and one more thing. They made me get rid of all the money!

By this time, I had a little more than three hundred dollars stashed away. Mom and Dad sat me down for a talk about what to do with my "ill-gotten gains," as Mom called them.

"We thought about making you give back the money to the kids who paid to bet," Mom said. "But we decided that it could get too complicated."

"Plus, those kids made some mistakes, too," Dad said. "They shouldn't have been betting in the first place."

I guess that's why they were waiting to talk to Mrs. Allegra.

It turned out they decided there was somebody who needed the money more than I did, or the other kids at Jonasburg Middle School did. Dad told me I was going to have to donate everything I'd earned off the gambling ring to a charity. "We have a few suggestions for you," he said, "if you need some ideas. Or you're welcome to come up with something on your own. But you're not going to keep that money."

You know, I wasn't too upset about that. *Making* the money had been fun. Figuring it all out—how to place the bets, how to eliminate the risk, how to make people want to give me two dollars every Monday. Having the money was fun, but it was never really the point.

I'm not sure Mom and Dad would have understood that, though. So I just nodded and agreed.

Thinking about where I'd donate all my cash was actually the only interesting thing that happened that whole week. Otherwise, one of those vocabulary words—"interminable"—basically described my days.

Boy, was it boring. And, worst of all, there was no one else to talk to.

At one point, my mind wandered and I reached for the phone in the living room to call Jamie. Then I remembered:

1) I wasn't allowed to use the phone.

2) Jamie hated my guts.

Still, I wondered what she was doing. Probably writing in her notebook. A new notebook, anyway. Maybe she was writing down more insults. *He's so dumb, he tried to drown a fish. She's so dumb, she tried to put M&M'S in alphabetical order.* Maybe she was reading her favorite magazine, *Sports Illustrated.* Maybe she was playing with Pepper. Maybe her parents had given her extra school assignments, too.

On Friday, when Dad asked if I wanted to go to the store with him, I was practically panting with excitement, just like Pepper when she thinks you're about to throw her ball.

Mom was working on some sort of "big secret project," and she had to go to Louisville to buy supplies. Dad was vague on the details but said that he had an appointment in the afternoon, and maybe I could "hold down the fort" while he was busy.

When I got to the store, I noticed that something looked different. There was a lot more *stuff* on display. Vases and paintings and teapots and sculptures and bowls. More of them than ever. One of the things on the walls was that painting I'd bought, the one-hundred-dollar one of the covered bridge. I remembered Mrs. Allegra saying that my parents had found it under my bed.

My dad saw me looking at it and walked over to the cash register. He took out a handful of twenties. "Here," he said. "The rest of the money—I know we said you had to donate it. But I think this is yours."

Oh, man. I felt sick.

It was weird. I'd been yelled at by the assistant principal and my best friend. I'd been suspended. I had to give away hundreds of dollars. But the thing that made me feel so bad that my stomach squirmed around inside me was when my dad made me take back that hundred dollars.

"No, Dad," I begged. "I don't want it. I don't. I just—I really wanted you to have it. Dad, please?"

He didn't budge. But after he pushed the money into my pocket, he leaned back against the counter and looked at me.

"You wanted us to have that money?" he asked softly.

I nodded.

"Why, Mitch?"

I'd told Jamie, but this was a lot tougher. How do you tell your dad that you're worried he and your mom aren't making enough money?

"I just—I was getting worried," I muttered, staring down at the floor. "That things were getting bad. Like back in California."

"Oh, Mitch."

Dad sounded so sad. That was really worse than him being mad. I looked quickly up at him and then down at the paint-splattered floor.

"I know it was rough on you, having to move," he said. "You and Kevin both. But things are okay here, right?"

"Yeah, things are okay," I agreed. That was sort of the point. "I just—I want them to keep on being okay, right, Dad? I like it here. I really do. I don't want to have to move again."

Dad sighed.

"Maybe I should get suspended, too," he said

sadly. "Mitch, really? Running an illegal gambling ring? You were worried about our family's finances, and *that* was your solution?"

Well, when he put it like that, it did sound kind of stupid.

"Listen," my dad said seriously. "You don't have to keep this family afloat. That's our job, your mom's and mine. Maybe we haven't always done it perfectly, but we're working on it. And it'll be okay. You're a kid. Please just *be* a kid. All right, Mitch?"

I must have made a face that indicated it wasn't all right.

"Mitch? Say what you're thinking, please. When you get that look on your face, I start to get worried you're about to go sell shares of the Brooklyn Bridge or start a gambling ring or something." He was smiling. But, I wasn't.

I took a deep breath.

"So I'm a kid. Right," I agreed. "But I do know some things, Dad. I do have good ideas."

"I know you do, Mitch."

"No, you don't!" He sort of jumped. I guess my

voice was a little loud. "When I try to talk about money, you don't ever listen. But I understand this stuff, Dad. I'm not trying to tell you about what glaze to put on your pots, or how hot to make the kiln. But I can help you sell stuff. Like—look at the store. Look at all this stuff!"

He looked around blankly. Like, *Yeah, there's a lot of stuff here. So?* "We've been hard at work making a lot of different things," he said. "Even if no one is buying them."

"Maybe that's not a coincidence."

Dad's eyebrows went up.

"Tell me more," he said. I hesitated. "No, really," he went on. "Are you saying that you think having more products to offer our customers, that show off more of our artistic talents, might be a *bad* thing?"

"Well, there is such a thing as too many choices," I said. "People get overwhelmed. Remember when Mom took me to get a Halloween costume last year and I eventually came home with nothing?"

"Yeah," said Dad.

"I couldn't decide because there were too many choices. There were hundreds and hundreds of costumes in the store. I could have been a zombie or an ax murderer or a mummy or a lumberjack or a racecar driver or a pirate or a hippie like you."

"If you'd chosen to be a hippie," he responded, "I could have given you your choice of tie-dyed shirts."

"But I didn't choose that. I didn't choose anything. It was way too much to think about. If there had been six costumes, I would have picked one. When there were six hundred, I was, like, frozen."

"If you were frozen, you should have gone as a yeti. Or the guy who drives the ice cream truck."

"Very funny," I said. "Seriously, Dad, sometimes less is more."

He nodded. He looked like he actually might have heard what I had to say. But right then the bell over the door jangled, and a serious-looking man carrying a binder full of files walked in. He reminded me of the guy the bank had sent to foreclose on our house in California.

"Mr. Collins!" Dad greeted him, shaking his hand. "The office is this way. Mitch, you're minding the shop. If you need anything, come get me."

CHAPTER 13

WHAT'S IT REALLY WORTH?

With Dad downstairs talking to Mr. Collins, I strolled around the shop. I was embarrassed to realize that I had never really looked at Mom's and Dad's artwork before. Sure, I'd seen it. But I'd never really appreciated it the way that I should have.

With nothing else to do, I studied the vases and pots and paintings. There was so much detail, all sorts of neat curlicues, intersecting lines, and colors I could swear I'd never seen before. I don't think that I'd ever felt prouder of Mom and Dad, even if all this art was still in the shop, unsold.

If you looked closely, there were even some jokes. Mom had made a painting of the bulls that live on the farm across the road from my grandma's house. On their cowbells, in the smallest letters, she had written their names: One was Kevin, the other was Mitch. Another of the oil paintings showed a boy going to school in Paris, with the Eiffel Tower in the background. She named it *French Schoolboy, Yves Dropper.*

Speaking of eavesdropping: When the Grateful Dead music Dad had put on the stereo got through its last track and stopped, the showroom got quieter and I could hear some of the discussion coming from downstairs. I could only pick up little bits of the conversation, but I sure didn't like what I heard—words like "renegotiate" and "penalty" and "debt."

I wanted to get closer, but figured I had already gotten in enough trouble for one week. Or month. Or year. Or for a kid's lifetime. Besides, just then the wind chimes over the door jingled. A customer!

A woman walked in, talking on her cell phone. She was wearing sunglasses and a Jonasburg baseball cap. "Yeah, I'm in Sloans' Creations," she said into her phone. "That new art store. Yeah, my kid is friends with the owners' kid. Lemme call you back."

Hmmm, I thought to myself. *She's the mom of which of Kevin's friends?* Neil Butwipe? Or maybe Julio Haberberg, the punter on the football team, who everyone says is worse than Clint Grayson, but who has been getting more action than he wants this season. Or maybe her "kid" is a girl and it's one of the sophomores or juniors who have a crush on Kevin.

Looking at this woman in her baseball cap made me think of Jamie. I tried to picture her as a grown-up. Maybe she would look like this woman when she got older. But no way would she ever wear those fancy designer sunglasses.

"What can I help you find?" I asked her, trying to sound as charming and professional as possible. This was another trick I had picked up from watching business shows and reading articles online.

When you walk into a store and the worker says, *Can I help you find anything?* it gives you the chance to say no. Politely, of course. But still, no is no. When you say, *What can I help you find?* you're kind of setting up the person to find *something.*

"Oh, a nice piece of art for our new living room," she said. "Something warm and inviting."

She strolled around the store, looking like an art critic. I thought about how weird it must be for my parents to have people come into their store, look at their work that they spent hours and hours, days and days, trying to make perfect, and then walk away. I'd be so tempted to say: *Wait, what don't you like about it? You think you could do better?*

The woman stopped right in front of the picture of the covered bridge. I kind of cringed inside.

"Wow," she said. "This is beautiful."

"It's great," I agreed. "Notice the shade of red on the roof?"

"Perfect," she gushed. "But it doesn't seem to have a price. How much is it?"

I probably should have gone downstairs, interrupted Dad, and asked. But instead I blurted out, "Well, what do you think it's worth?"

See, if you want to buy something like a pizza or an airline ticket, you can figure out a fair price by checking around. But with art, it's different. It's not like there's another store selling paintings of covered bridges. Or maybe there is, but not exactly like *this* painting. Each piece of art is unique, one of a kind. So the price is unique, too.

"Oh, gosh, I don't know," she replied. "Maybe three hundred dollars?"

Sweet!

"I think that's fair," I said.

"Don't you want to check with your folks first?" she asked.

"Nah, they trust me," I said, trying my hardest to sound grown-up.

"Yes, we do," said Dad's voice.

I jumped. I hadn't even heard him come up from the office. But there he was, leaning in the doorway, grinning at me and the customer.

"Mitch is in charge of the business end," he said.

"Couldn't handle things without him. Let me get that wrapped up for you."

When Dad had her painting safely wrapped and she was about to go, I asked her something. "I heard you talking on the phone when you walked in. Who's your kid, the one who's friends with Kevin?"

"Kevin?" she asked. "I don't know Kevin. My son says he's friends with you."

Friends? With me?

"My name is Catherine Barnes," she said. "My son is Ben."

"Nice to meet you, Mrs. Barnes," I said, holding out my hand. "I like Ben a lot, too."

"A pleasure," she said, shaking my hand. "Ben told me that you're really smart and clever." She smiled. "And it's nice to see you putting those smarts to *good* use this time."

Uh-oh. Was I about to get yelled at by another adult? "I'm sorry if I got Ben in trouble. I didn't mean to...."

"It's okay," she said. "No one else got suspended. The school just gave every participant a stern warning. And Ben knows he did something wrong, too. He's not blameless."

"Well, please tell him I said hi."

"You can tell him yourself," she said with a smile. "He'd like to hear from you." She started to walk out, then paused and turned around. "But just to be clear, you're not going to start another scheme—"

"No way!" my dad and I shouted at the same time before she could even finish.

═══

The Sunday night before I went back to school, life started to feel normal again. Mom and Dad gave me back my TV and Internet privileges. Once I finished the last of my homework, put out my clothes, and packed my lunch, I could watch football. But after everything that happened, I realized I wasn't as excited to watch as I used to be.

I also knew things were getting back to normal when Kevin asked for a loan again, complaining that he had blown through his weekly allowance.

"I only need a few dollars," he whined. "It's for lunch tomorrow. I'll pay you back. With interest."

I was tempted to use a line from the Shakespeare play *Hamlet*. Some of my homework over the last four days had been to try to read it. I didn't really understand much, but this one line made a lot of sense: *"Neither a borrower nor a lender be. For loan oft loses both itself and friend, and borrowing dulls the edge of husbandry."*

I was pretty confused at first because I thought "husbandry" probably had something to do with being a "husband." But then I looked up the definition and found out that it means "working hard." The whole line basically says: When you borrow or lend money, you can lose both money *and* friends. Kind of like when you make bets, I guess. Plus, borrowing money (and maybe winning bets, too) makes you less willing to work hard.

But I didn't quote Shakespeare at Kevin. For one thing, you know how I was feeling about money right then? Kind of like a guy who's just won a hot dog eating contest would feel about hot dogs. *Ugh. No thanks, no more.* I found a balled-up five-dollar

bill in my pocket and tossed it to Kevin. "Keep it,"
I said.

"Hey, thanks, Mitch," he said in a low voice,
sounding extra grateful.

"I'll give you a tip, too," I said.

"It's okay," Kevin said. "I just need a few bucks.
You don't have to give me more than that."

"No, not that kind of a tip," I said. "A tip like free
advice."

"What's that?"

"When you get your allowance this week, ask
for it in one-dollar bills. Then get seven envelopes,
one for each day of the week, and put three dollars
in each envelope. You have three dollars to spend
each day. Do that and you won't spend all your
money before the seventh day."

Before he could respond, Mom walked into
the room and handed me a bag. "Your father and
I wanted you to have this present, since Indiana's
going to be our new home for a while."

She looked at me like she wanted to be sure I'd
heard that last part of the sentence: "for a while."
Still, I thought this might be some sort of joke,

seeing as how presents are usually rewards. And I hadn't exactly done much in recent days to deserve a reward. I opened the bag anyway, and it was an Indiana Hoosiers basketball jersey.

"Dad and I figured that since you're going back to school and starting fresh, you should be wearing something new and fresh."

"Thanks, Mom," I said. "That was really cool of you."

"And groovy of Dad, right?"

I laughed for the first time in what seemed like forever.

As I walked into school on Monday, I was more nervous than I'd been on the first day of classes way back in August. Knowing how fast gossip bounces around the walls here, I was sure that tales of the Rookie Bookie, his gambling, his bust, and his suspension had already made the rounds.

After Dad dropped me in front of the main entrance, I walked quickly along the B corridor staring at my shoes. Kind of like I used to do in California. I wanted to get to my locker and then right to class.

Nobody yelled my name, nobody high-fived me. And it was the first time in a lot of Mondays that there wasn't a crowd gathered around my locker to greet me.

Actually, they were never really there to greet me. They'd been there to get paid.

I wasn't exactly surprised that Jamie wasn't there either.

The first two periods whizzed by. Then it was time for math. It seemed like a lot more than a week had gone by since I last saw Mr. Rafferty standing before the class. Today, he looked like he had a personal grudge against fashion. (He was wearing a black jacket with patches on the elbows, gray corduroy pants, and a turtleneck shirt the color of applesauce.)

When the bell sounded and the class grew quiet, he stared right at me. Well, not stared. He looked at me as if he was glad to see me.

"Mitch, are you unhappy to be back with us in math class?" he asked.

What did he mean by that? Why would he bring up the fact that I had been suspended?

"Um, what?" I asked. "What do you mean?"

"Are you unhappy to be back in class?"

"No," I said uneasily.

"Hear that, everyone?" Mr. R. said, his voice rising with excitement. "Mitch is *not un*happy to be here. So, that's good. He's glad to be here. And we're happy to see you, Mitch."

That's nice, I thought, *but where's he going with this?*

"Someone who is *not unhappy* is happy. The same way someone who is *not thoughtless* is thoughtful. Or someone who did *not disappear* is here. And someone who is *not malnourished* is fed just fine. Two negatives make a positive. And the same holds true in the wild and wonderful world of mathcmatics."

He then went on to explain that negative four times negative seven is positive twenty-eight (−4 x −7 = 28) and that eleven minus negative eight is positive nineteen (11 − −8 = 19).

Not bad to be back with you, Mr. R., I thought to myself.

At lunch, I walked right by some of the kids who had hung around my locker and fist-bumped me on Monday mornings. Now they pretended like they had never seen me before. You know those songs they play on the radio that are popular for a while, but then sort of fall out of the rotation? That's how I felt.

But as I sat down at an empty table near the milk dispenser and ate my slices of pizza alone, I realized that I was okay with it. Weird, but true. It had been fun being the guy everybody talked to about bets and money and football, but, deep down, all those kids had been more interested in winning eighteen dollars than getting to know me. And I kind of knew it all along, even if I'd ignored it for a while.

"Hey, Mitch," somebody said, and Ben Barnes flopped down in the seat across from me. He was digging into a bag of Cheetos and licking his orange fingers. "Want some?" He waved the bag at me.

"No, thanks," I said, but I grinned.

"Did your mom really do that painting of the bridge? The one my mom bought?"

"Yeah, she did."

"That's cool. It's really good."

Wow. Ben didn't seem mad at all. I guess his mom was right.

I popped open my ginger ale. "Yeah, she is really good. I'll tell her you liked it."

Maybe everything was going to be okay. Maybe not everybody hated me and I really could start fresh like Mom said.

But that good feeling disappeared as soon as I looked across the lunchroom and saw Jamie come in by herself. I tried to catch her eye, but she headed for a corner of the room as far away from our usual table as she could get.

CHAPTER 14

RISK AND REWARD

During the week I was home from school, Mom and Dad had talked with Mrs. Allegra about how I could do "restitution" (that had been one of my vocabulary words from Mom; it means to pay back). Mrs. Allegra thought I could reshelve library books or organize the lost-and-found. But Dad asked, "Is there any chance there's something Mitch could do that's sports-related?"

So Mrs. Allegra decided I could use seventh period, my study hall time, to clean up the locker rooms that the football teams used, both the middle school and high school. "The middle school locker room is a pigsty," she said with a disgusted look. "And the high school locker room is just as bad."

I thought she was exaggerating, but boy was I wrong. It was far, far worse than a pigsty. After sixth period, I headed down the stairs to the school's athletic annex. I wasn't even at the bottom before an awful smell washed over me. It was a mix of sweat and mildew and dirt and something else. Maybe a dead goat. Even Clint Grayson's Dorito breath was ten times better than this.

I'm not sure why, but I had pictured the football team's locker room to be a glamorous place. I imagined carpet on the floor and big-screen TVs mounted on the walls and whiteboards for the coaches to use when they diagrammed plays. Instead it was just like the locker room we used in gym class. Only it smelled worse.

The custodian was waiting for me. It sounds mean to say, but Mr. Eads looked a little bit like a troll. He was short with big ears and a big nose and wore flannel shirts with the sleeves rolled up. There was a rumor that he lived in a secret apartment on school grounds.

"Follow me," he said, staring at the floor.

Without exchanging any more words, Mr. Eads and I went to work sweeping up the locker-room floors. There were yards and yards of athletic tape stuck to it, empty bottles of Gatorade, used bandages, used Kleenexes. There were pennies, mouth guards caked with dust, dirty wristbands, hand towels, clumps of grass, and what was either a very large cornflake or a scab. It was gross.

When we finished, Mr. Eads motioned for me to follow him. We went down a back staircase where the largest washing machine and clothes dryer I had ever seen were waiting. Never mind clothes; you could wash and dry the entire team in them. Mr. Eads unloaded all the uniforms from the dryer, threw them on a table, and showed me how to fold the jerseys and the pants.

There was something a little bit humiliating about picking up the trash left by the football players and then folding their uniforms. But maybe that was part of the point of this. It was a punishment, right? I kept my mouth shut, anyway. Complaining about it might have been kind of annoying to Mr. Eads, since this wasn't a punishment for him; it was his regular job.

And just like my suspension, it was getting boring really quickly. Mr. Eads sure didn't seem like he was going to start up any small talk to pass the time. So, it was up to me.

"Wow, you really know what you're doing," I said, trying my hardest.

"Been at it for more than twenty years," he replied. "I oughta know by now."

And he stopped talking. Up to me again.

"My brother, Kevin, is a wide receiver on the high school team," I said. "Did you see that great catch he made against Gas City? The one where they called holding and the touchdown didn't count?"

"Not hardly." He laughed. "My bowling league meets every Friday, so I can't go to the football games even if I wanted to."

I was running out of conversation topics.

"I know from my brother that these uniforms get pretty dirty every week," I said.

"Team's not good this year, huh?"

"No, they're not so good," I said. "You heard?"

"Not really. But you said your brother plays offense and his uniform gets dirty," he said. "A lot of dirt on the uniforms means that the boys are spending a lot of time on the ground. Which is never a good sign when it's your job to score touchdowns."

Wow, I'd never thought of it that way. Other kids could make fun of Mr. Eads, but he was doing something that clever people in business do all the time—using what he could see to figure out what he couldn't.

Jonasburg was a good example of this. When we moved to our new town, I was curious if the area would be growing and successful so Mom and Dad would have a better shot with their business. Were other people and businesses moving here? Or were we going to a place where everything was shrinking and businesses were moving away?

When we drove around, I noticed a lot of cranes

and buildings under construction. That was a good sign that Mom and Dad had moved us to a place where they might have a chance. Even though I couldn't see the town's growing businesses directly, I knew they must be doing well or else I wouldn't have seen all the new construction sites.

Mr. Eads and I continued folding in silence until he surprised me with a question. "Are you the boy who was doing the gambling on the football games?"

"I wasn't exactly doing the gambling," I answered. "I was organizing the . . . wait, how'd you hear about that?"

"One thing about this place," Mr. Eads replied, "word travels fast."

I waited for him to ask another question, but that seemed to be it for our small talk. Oh, well. We were going to be spending a lot of time together, Mr. Eads and I. We'd have time for more later.

I carried the uniforms for the middle school team upstairs, and Mr. Eads followed with the high school's. As I turned the corner, I heard voices coming from the locker room, which meant that the players were starting to file in. If I had listened more closely, I would have recognized one particular voice and turned the other way.

It was Clint Grayson. He was holding a Gatorade bottle, and he saw me immediately.

"Is that who I think it is? Little Mitchy? Shouldn't you be suspended or something?" He laughed.

As usual, the kids around him joined in even though he said nothing that was especially funny. It was almost like they were hoping he would continue picking on me and not pick on them instead. And the laughing only made him try harder, like cheers from the crowd at a football game.

"What are you doing here? I know it's not for football, because you weren't good enough to make the team." He grinned widely.

It seemed like anything I could say would just make things worse. The truth is, I didn't want to have to talk to him at all. Could I just walk by with my pile of uniforms? No, he was blocking my way.

"Maybe you got deaf during your suspension," he said more seriously. "I asked you a question: What are you doing here?"

This is something else I hate about bullies: They tongue-tie you. Later, you think of a good comeback. *What am I doing here, Clint? I asked a GPS to help me locate the dumbest seventh grader in the entire state of Indiana. And it sent me to your locker.* But when they're in your face, you can't think of a snappy comeback.

"I'm cleaning up the locker room," I said flatly.

"Guess you're sorry now that you didn't give me that free bet, huh?"

Wait a minute. What did Clint just say?

Boy, did I feel like an idiot. I was supposed to be the smart one, and I'd missed all the clues.

Clint had told me I'd be sorry for not letting him bet for free.

Mrs. Allegra had said "a concerned student" had found Jamie's notebook and given it to her.

Concerned. Yeah, right. Concerned about getting back at me!

"You gave that notebook to Mrs. Allegra!" I exploded. "You—you—" All my words got jammed up in my throat. There were plenty of things I wanted to call Clint Grayson. But yelling them in the locker room was likely to get me an even longer suspension.

And he grinned at me like he knew exactly what I wanted to call him, and he didn't care. "Cleaning up the locker room, huh?" he said. "Clean *this* up, then!"

He opened the cap of his Gatorade and poured out the contents. Sticky yellow liquid splattered all over the floor. Of course, it was met with a chorus of laughs, and my face turned even redder.

In less than a minute, Clint had managed to ruin what had otherwise been a pretty good first day back at school.

The next day after sixth period, I walked down to the locker room again. When I didn't see Mr. Eads, I went down to the laundry and started to fold the uniforms by myself.

I had only done a few when a voice called, "Eads, is that you?"

"No, it's Sloan," I responded. I figured it was a

locker room thing, calling everyone by their last name.

"Kevin?" came the voice again, sounding puzzled.

"No, Mitch."

The footsteps got louder down the stairs, and then I saw that it was Coach Williams.

"Oh, hey, Coach," I said, "I'm—"

"I remember you. Kevin's kid brother. You're the kid who had those suggestions for me during football tryouts. If you could play football half as well as you think football, you would've made the team, easy."

I wasn't sure if this was a compliment or an insult, but I thanked him anyway.

"How's the punishment working for you?" Coach Williams asked.

"You heard?"

"Yeah, not many secrets around this place," he said. "You were running some kind of gambling ring, right? Got suspended, and now you're like a prisoner on work release, cleaning up this dump. You have my sympathy." He paused for a second. "Then again, at least you're not about to get fired."

There really weren't many secrets.

"Been a rough fall for both of us," I said.

"You can say that again," said Coach Williams, his voice dropping an octave. "Let me ask you something: You been to many of our games?"

"Sure," I said.

"What do you think of the job the head coach has been doing?"

I wasn't sure if he wanted me to say something nice or to give him an honest answer.

"Well," I said, "I know my brother and his friends on the team love playing for you."

"But that's not what I asked," he said, smiling. "I remember from the tryouts how smart you are. Shoot straight with me: How do you think I've been doing?"

Okay, he'd asked for honesty. "Some of your decisions don't always make a lot of sense to me."

"Give me an example," he said, shifting his weight from one foot to the other.

I paused, trying to think of an easy one. "Remember the game against Ikeville, when they were leading 13-0, we scored to make it 13-6, and you decided to go for a two-point conversion instead of kicking an extra point?"

"Sure," he said.

"Well, to me—and my friend Jamie, too—that didn't make much sense."

"I just felt in my gut that we could catch them off guard. And two points is better than one, right?"

"Yeah, but here's the problem," I said. "The chances of getting the one point are better than the chances of getting the two points. And even if you *had* gotten the two points, that would only have made the score 13–8. If you'd kicked the extra point it would have been 13–7. So either way, Jonasburg would have needed another touchdown to win. Going for the two points was more risk, but it didn't get you any more reward."

He nodded his head slowly. "I get it now."

Behind him, the players were starting to file in. I could tell immediately that he didn't want them overhearing their coach getting advice from a middle schooler.

"I got a practice to run, but I appreciate this," he

said. "If you think of any more examples, lay 'em on me. I got thick skin. You have to, in this job."

"You got it, Coach," I said.

"Oh, one more thing, Little Sloan," he said. "Thanks for being honest with me."

———

"Mitch, phone's for you."

Huh? Wha? I was fast asleep on Saturday when Dad came bursting into my room. In one motion, he woke me up and handed me the phone. "It's for you. And it's time to get up."

"Hello?" I said into the phone, my first word of the day.

It was Ben Barnes. And he was inviting me to go to the mall in Louisville with him.

"Um, maybe," I said. "What do you need to buy?"

He started laughing and explained that he didn't need to buy anything. Going to the mall was just something to do in Indiana. You walk around. You see if anyone else is there from your school. You look at the kids from other schools. You go to the arcade. You get an Icee drink or a slice of pizza from the food court. You go to Sports King and get ideas for your holiday wish list.

Honestly, it sounded kind of boring. Why would you want to go to a mall and just walk around? We never did that in San Francisco. On the other hand, I was happy Ben thought to invite me. "Let me ask my parents, but I think I can go," I told him. "Yeah, it'll be fun."

And it actually was. Mrs. Barnes drove us. When she picked me up, she insisted on coming inside the house to meet "the extraordinary artist" who also happened to be my mom.

"It's so nice to finally meet you. I can't tell you how much I admire your work," she said, sounding like a fan meeting a rock star she worshipped. "Your painting looks lovely in my living room. Already I've had three friends ask where I got it. With any luck, I'll be sending some business your way."

"Well, thanks," Dad said, covering for Mom, who seemed embarrassed. "Mitch always said that word of mouth is important for a small business like ours—it can make you or break you."

"Oh, and Mitch—he was a great salesman!" Mrs. Barnes went on. Now I was getting embarrassed. "Speaking of word of mouth," she went on, "I organize a benefit for the Jonasburg schools every year. You don't have to give me an answer right now, but we would love it if you wanted to donate a painting or a piece of pottery for the auction."

With Mom and Dad left to think about that, we said our good-byes and headed down Route 26. As we pulled into the huge parking lot of the Galaxy Mall, I realized that ever since I got busted for running the gambling pool, my supply of cash had really dwindled. Between donating my "ill-gotten gains," giving money to Kevin, and paying for school lunches, I didn't have a whole lot left to spend.

Ben seemed to have plenty, though, so we made a plan to meet Mrs. Barnes at the Electronics Hothouse in three hours.

We wandered all over and eventually ended up at Sports King, the biggest sporting-goods store I had ever been to. There were posters of famous athletes on the walls, and at least a dozen TV monitors showing different sports programs. Ben went to the section that sold baseball bats, and he took some practice swings. I stayed closer to the front of the store, looking at all the running shoes. Most of the clothes I wore were Kevin's hand-me-downs, but at least I could get my own shoes.

As I stared at a pair of black high-tops with white stripes and a secret zipper under the tongue, I heard a girl arguing with her mother in the aisle behind me.

"Can we get out of this store already and get you something more appropriate?" the mom said.

"Wait—let me just see if they've got the new Atlanta Braves caps," the girl said.

"You have nice hair and you're mashing it under a baseball hat," the mom said. "I think it's time for the sports phase to pass. Time to start dressing more like a teenage girl and less like a tomboy."

"I like the way I dress," the girl said. "And the skirt you just showed me was hideous. It was so ugly it hurt my eyes."

Wait a second.

I peered around the corner, and, yes, it was Jamie Spielberger, arguing with her mother. I saw her right away and she saw me. Then she turned away so fast she could have gotten whiplash. "Whatever, Mom," she said. "Fine. Let's just get out of here. This store has gotten totally lame."

What had been a fun afternoon had just gotten less fun. And I didn't feel like telling Ben the whole story. *I just saw Jamie. I got this weird feeling. We saw each other, but she turned and walked out of the store. Yes, I know she's still mad at me. No, I don't like her. Well, I like her, but not that way. Yes, you're right that I probably shouldn't care.*

So I kept it to myself.

CHAPTER 15

THERE'S NO RULE AGAINST HAVING BETTER INFORMATION

At three o'clock we met Ben's mom. She was buying Mr. Barnes an early Christmas gift, a pair of binoculars he could use when he went bird-watching. As Mrs. Barnes paid, the sales clerk asked if she wanted an extended warranty for twelve extra dollars.

"What's that?" Mrs. Barnes asked.

"Well, if anything goes wrong with your product," he said, "and you have an extended warranty, we'll cover it."

"Don't do it," I said.

"No?" she said. "Why?"

"For a lot of reasons," I said. "First of all, the binoculars already come with a warranty. It says so right on the box. Second, do binoculars really break that often? You'd be paying almost twenty-five percent of the price for the warranty and probably will never use it. And, if you don't get the warranty and it does break, replacing the binoculars is not that expensive. Also, just because you have the warranty doesn't mean you'll be able to find it when you want to use it. It's like those gift cards. Basically it's a rip-off."

Mrs. Barnes looked at the clerk. "My advisor says no, so I think I'll pass," she said with a smile.

"Suit yourself," he said in a voice that suggested that, deep down, he knew the extended warranty was a rip-off, too.

"Man, you know a lot about this kind of stuff," Ben said as we walked to the car. "When I get rich and famous, you can definitely be the guy who handles my money."

I kind of liked that idea, helping rich and famous

people manage their money. It was a job I could see myself doing. I knew I'd told Mrs. Barnes the right thing about the warranty, and she'd listened. Mom and Dad were maybe going to listen to me, too, about business ideas.

It got me thinking, after Ben and his mom dropped me off, about helping people. Cleaning up the locker room was one thing. But anybody could do that. Even that idiot Clint Grayson.

There might be something else I could do to help. To pay back. Something that most people wouldn't be able to do—but I could.

That Monday, when I got to the locker room and folded uniforms with Mr. Eads during study hall, I had my ear out for Coach Williams. I heard him coming into the locker room, and I asked Mr. Eads if I could have a quick break.

"Sure, take off for the day," he said. "We're about finished here. It goes faster with two people, that's for sure."

"Hey, it's Little Sloan," Coach Williams said when I found him. He was sitting on one of the locker room benches, and he looked really tired. "Got any more tips for an old man?"

I didn't really like that nickname, but that was something for later. Right now I had this idea, and it was about to come bursting out of my mouth.

"You ever use statistics?" I asked eagerly. "When you're thinking about what plays to run, or the strategy for a game?"

The coach shrugged.

"I go by my gut, mostly," he said, not really looking at me. "Lots of experience up here." He tapped his forehead with one finger. "But sometimes I check to see a few things. How often the other team runs the football, how often they pass. Stuff like that."

"Basic stuff," I said.

"I suppose."

"And it makes no sense," I barreled on. Now the coach did look up at me, a little startled. I guess I was about to be annoying. But you know what? He needed it.

"Why not look at *all* the statistics? I mean, as

much as you can? There's no rule against having more information than the other team, right?"

That's almost exactly what I'd said to Jamie, the first time I won the bet against her. And I'd said it to Kevin, too. Maybe he had a point about how the other kids in the betting ring didn't know it was a competition, didn't know they should have been using their brains against mine.

But a football game? *Everybody* knows that's a competition. Everybody knows each team is doing all they can to win.

So I said it again, to Coach Williams. "There's no rule against having more information than Clarksville, is there?"

Coach Williams shook his head. "Mitch, I appreciate it. I really do. But I don't have time to find out all the numbers, not before this weekend."

"I know," I said. "But I do."

———

I knew I couldn't do it alone, so just like every weekend for months, I called my partner.

Unlike every other weekend, she hung up on me.

I called her back. "Jamie, wait a minute!"

She hung up again.

I called her back again. "Seriously, Spielberger, knock it off!" I barked before she could slam the phone down. "Listen to me! I've got to say something to you, and I'm not calling again!"

There was a really, really long silence, then Jamie's voice. "Okay. I'm listening."

"I need your help with something," I told her.

"You are kidding, Sloan. Kidding. Right? And you're not even funny."

"Hey, back off, will you?" I was starting to get a little mad, too. "I know we got into trouble, and I'm sorry, but "

"But? You're sorry, *but*? Your sorry butt better come up with a better apology than that if you want some help from me!"

"Hey!" This was not how I'd wanted this conversation to go at all. But I didn't seem to have any control over it. I'd known for a couple of weeks that Jamie was seriously mad at me, and now, all of a sudden, I was finding out I was mad at her, too.

I knew the gambling was my idea. I knew she'd kind of wanted to quit before we got into trouble, and I'd talked her into keeping it going.

But that didn't mean it was *all* my fault, every single thing that had happened.

"What's this about, Jamie? I didn't *make* you take the bets! You wanted to do it, too! You came up with half the ideas! Why are you acting like I started World War III all by myself?"

"You said we wouldn't get into trouble! I *trusted* you, Mitch."

"Well—sorry." There. I said it.

"And I wanted to stop, and you wouldn't let me!"

"Wouldn't *let* you? Come on, Jamie! I'm not some big bad guy with a machine gun over here! If you'd really wanted to quit, you would have!"

"How was I supposed to, after you told me all that stuff about your family and how you needed the money and everything?" Her voice sounded different than I'd ever heard it before. Like she was going to cry.

The idea made me feel less mad, and more panicky. I didn't want to hear Jamie cry.

"How was I supposed to just say forget it when you needed my help? How was I supposed to turn my back on a friend?"

Oh. Wow.

I felt just about as bad as I had when Dad gave me that hundred dollars back. I break about half the rules in school and get suspended and everything, and the thing that really makes me feel like dog crap is when somebody gives me money, and somebody else calls me a friend.

So I did the only thing I could think to do.

"Sorry, Jamie. Really. I didn't think it was going to be this bad. I honestly didn't." I sighed. "If you want me to vanish off the face of the earth, I will. Maybe they'll move my locker if I ask. I could change my last name to Ackerman or Baker or something if you want."

Jamie sniffled. Loud. "Don't be an idiot, Sloan."

That seemed to be a slightly hopeful sign.

"Anyway. Say hi to Pepper for me, okay? And never mind, I won't ask for your help with this thing. I guess that was really stupid, thinking you'd want to help me out. I mean, it's for Coach

Williams, too, and the football team, so it's not just for me. But I won't bother you. Forget it."

"I *said*, don't be an idiot. What do you need me to do?"

═══

Jamie came over to my place, right after I'd explained my idea. She said her parents would not be too excited about the idea of me turning up at their house. "My mom really liked you at first," she explained, getting off her bike. "She probably thought you'd take me to the seventh-grade dance or something. But right now you're not her favorite person."

Whoa. My brain went into free fall there for a second. All of a sudden I saw Jamie in a dress with one of those strange little bouquets of flowers tied to her wrist, and me in a suit. Like I even *own* a suit. It was a very disturbing image, and I shook it off because she was staring at me like I'd grown an extra head.

"Are we getting to work here or what?" she demanded.

I'd printed out all the information I could find, and all I could get from Coach Williams, too. We were going to look at all the stats from Jonasburg's games. And we were going to look at all of Clarksville's games. Every game, every play. We were going to be in information overload.

What plays were the most and least successful? What kinds of defenses worked best? In which quarter did Jonasburg score the most points and the least? Were there certain penalties that the team was most likely to commit—our team, or the other one? Was Jonasburg more successful throwing the ball to the right side of the field, the left side, or the middle?

Coach Williams had gotten me DVDs and video links of the games, and Jamie and I drank organic ginger ale and chomped our way through bags of chips as we watched. I made up a spreadsheet to keep track of everything we were discovering.

We were discovering a *lot*. Like this:

- When Neil threw a pass on first down, he seemed to catch the defense off guard. Throughout the season, he had completed less than half his passes, only forty-eight percent. But when he threw the ball on first down, he threw a completion more than seventy percent of the time.

- When Jonasburg ran the ball to the right side of the field, they averaged less than one yard. When they ran to the left side, they gained more than five yards. When they ran on third down, which was rare, they gained six to seven yards.
- On average, Jonasburg gained eleven yards for every kickoff return. The three times during the season that Kevin returned a kickoff, he averaged twenty-nine yards.
- Clarksville hadn't been called for a single pass interference penalty all season.
- Clarksville has passed the ball on almost every single third down this season.
- Ninety-two percent of Clarksville's punts landed on the right side of the field.

"It's better than fantasy football," Jamie murmured, peering over my shoulder at the computer.

"It's *real* football. It actually means something, you know?"

"I guess that's a good way to look at it," I said. "Especially if it can save Coach Williams from getting fired."

There was so much I wanted to say to her. But it was like the sugar that gets stuck on the side of the shaker. Nothing came out. Luckily, Jamie kept on talking.

"So," she said. "How much trouble did you get in, anyway?"

"I don't know. Medium, I guess. Extra chores at home while I was suspended. And one day I had to work at my parents' store."

But the really bad thing...I looked over at her. Should I tell her?

I remembered her voice on the phone. Yeah. I should tell her. I explained how my dad had handed me back the money I'd spent on that painting, and how it had made me feel. She whistled.

"But they made me give away the rest of the money," I added. "And I decided to donate that hundred dollars, too. So I'm broke now. Remember how much money we made? I might have to borrow from Kevin pretty soon."

"Tell me about it," she said. "My parents said I had to put all the money into a college fund. So I've got nothing left. I used to find crumpled up twenty-dollar bills in the pockets of my pants. Now I'm happy if I find a few pennies in the back of my dresser drawer. Who'd you give your money to?"

"Actually, I didn't give it away," I told her. "I loaned it instead."

"Mitch? Seriously? What are you doing, charging interest? You think that might get you in trouble again?"

"Not the way I did it." I pulled up a webpage on the computer to show her. "It's this site, see? You can donate money, and they loan it to people all over the world. If somebody wants to, I don't know, sell bananas or something. Or buy a cow so they can sell the milk. These people might have a really good idea to make their lives a lot better, but they just need a little bit of money to get it started. Then they pay it back, and you loan it to somebody else. Check it out."

She read a few of the stories on the site, and grinned. "Cool. That's better than a college fund."

"I loaned this guy money for a new engine for his boat. He's paid some of it back already," I told her. This part actually didn't feel like a punishment at all. It was a lot of fun seeing how my loans did, and imagining some dude named Ronnie, halfway around the world, catching fish every day, fish that he could sell, because of the money that I loaned him.

"So how about you?" I asked Jamie. "How much trouble did you get into?"

"It was weird," she said. "My mom freaked out. But I think it's mostly because she didn't really get it. *'If you had passed notes in class or tried to wear short skirts, the way we did when I was in school, it would be one thing. But betting on football?'*"

I had only been around Mrs. Spielberger a few times, but I could tell Jamie was doing a good imitation of her.

Jamie continued: "My dad was different. He tried to act all angry in front of my mom but I could tell he wasn't that upset. One time he even let it slip: *'That sounds like the kind of thing I would have done at your age.'*"

It was another good imitation.

"I'll never be the son he wanted me to be. But it's, like, if I do things a boy would normally do—no matter how bad—he doesn't really mind. Maybe I'll start belching and spitting gigantic loogeys."

"You already do that," I said.

"Shut up," she said. Then she smiled.

And we kept talking. Like normal. Pretty soon we were even laughing about the day we got caught. "I still picture Mrs. Allegra calling me Mitchell and gripping her pen like it was a sword and she wanted to poke me!" I told her.

"Oh, I know!" said Jamie. "I think I even saw a little spit coming out of the corners of her mouth. She was like a rabid dog."

"When she was yelling at me, there were veins popping out on her neck. She was staring at me so hard, I'm surprised her makeup didn't crack right off her face."

"Good one!" said Jamie, reaching into her back

pocket and pulling out a notebook. "I have to write that down. I'm going to use it!"

"What do you mean 'use it'?" I asked.

"Oh, I'm writing a book about our, um, adventure," she said. "It started when I was suspended and then grounded, too. I started to write down everything that had happened and the words kept coming out."

"It *is* a pretty good story."

"You're telling me. Who knows? I may even write it in your voice."

"What are you calling it?"

"I'm thinking about *The Rookie Bookie*."

"Nice," I said. "Just do us both one favor: Don't leave that notebook hanging around where people can find it."

CHAPTER 16

PART OF THE TEAM

After Jamie had to leave, I was collecting our notes and empty ginger ale cans when Dad poked his head into the room. "What are you up to?" he said, so I explained about my brilliant plan to help Jonasburg beat Clarksville.

"Hmmm," he said. "Sounds like surreptitious skullduggery."

"What*ever*," I said.

"Oh, I forgot to tell you," he said, changing the

subject. "Your mother and I are going out tonight. Kevin is babysitting."

"No, he's not," I corrected him. "Unless you and Mom have a third child I don't know about, there are no *babies* who need *sitting*. Kevin and I both happen to be home alone tonight and he just happens to be older. That's all."

"What*ever*," Dad said, making fun of me. "And don't be so concerned with titles. It makes you seem like you're a part of Corporate America, working for The Man."

"What-EV-er. Where are you guys going to tonight, anyway?" I asked.

"It's that PTA benefit for the school," he said. "Mom made a huge statue of a whale, for the Jonasburg Whales, that they're going to auction off."

They left about a half hour later, and boy, did they look different. Dad was wearing a shirt that had a collar and no writing on it, a belt around his waist, pants that weren't jeans, and shoes that weren't made of canvas. Mom's hair was all neat, she was wearing a dress, and she had on lipstick.

So it was just me and Kevin. (Or Kevin and me.)

When people ask me, "Do you get along with your brother?" I roll my eyes and wrinkle up my nose. I suspect Kevin does the same thing when he gets asked about me. But the truth is, deep down, I actually...well, put it this way: It could be a lot worse. And I especially like Kevin (there, I said it) when we're home alone.

I couldn't wait to show him some of the "nuggets" about his team that Jamie and I had dug up. "Look," I said. "Your team has been called for only one holding penalty all year! Tell the guys on the offensive line they need to be more aggressive! And, look here: Clarksville has been called for seventeen offside penalties this season. Seventeen!"

Kevin didn't share my enthusiasm.

"Maybe you don't understand this because you don't play football," he said. "But when another guy is trying to tackle you and grind you into the ground, you're not thinking about the 'percentage of this' and 'number of times that' and all the other nerd stuff. No offense."

But I wasn't done. "Kevin, if I told you that saying a certain word, or wearing a certain color shirt, or wearing a certain kind of cologne, would give you a better chance of impressing a pretty girl, would you do it? It wouldn't guarantee anything, but it would give you a better chance."

"Probably," he said, shrugging. "Yeah, sure."

"But you're not thinking about statistics and numbers and 'nerd stuff' when you talk to girls, are you?"

"Okay," he sighed. "I get your point."

I showed him the sheets I had printed and we started "geeking out" (that's what Kevin called it) over the nuggets.

"I'm telling you, Mitch, this is almost like cheating," he said.

"But it's not," I assured him. "All this information is floating around out there, available to anyone."

"If," said Kevin arching his eyebrow and grinning, "they know where to look."

We gave each other a high five.

———

Mom and Dad hadn't looked much like Mom and Dad when they'd left home. But when they got back, I barely recognized them.

I was awake in bed, but even if I had been asleep, they would have woken me up. They barged in and were almost yelling with excitement.

"Mitch, we did it!" said Dad. "We listened to your advice and we did it!"

"Huh? Did what? Listened how?"

"At the auction!" he said. I swear he was almost hyperventilating.

"What?"

Mom cut Dad off. "Before the auction started, they asked us what the statue was worth. Where should they start the bidding? I was going to give them a number, but then I remembered what you always said: *Something is worth what another person is willing to pay for it.*"

"So we didn't say anything," Dad explained. "We just told them to start taking bids."

"And then it got interesting," Mom said. "They showed a photo of the statue on the screen and everyone gasped. One man with slicked-back hair and these fancy eyeglasses said, 'Ten thousand dollars!' People got really excited, and the auctioneer started banging his gavel. Before he did the whole 'going once, going twice' thing, a woman in the fanciest dress I've ever seen shouted, 'Fifteen thousand dollars!' "

"Whoa," said Kevin, who had entered the room. "You could buy a car for that much money."

Dad kept going. "This man and this woman were on opposite sides of the room and they were going back and forth, driving up the price. The whole audience was cheering, like they were watching a football game."

"Finally the two bidders made an agreement," Mom said, taking over again. "They would both buy it, put both their names on it, and donate it to the school. So from now on, everyone walking through the front door will walk past the King-Montgomery whale statue, created by yours truly, Janet Sloan."

"Cool!" Kevin and I said together.

"How much did it finally go for?" I asked.

"Art has no price," Mom said, sticking her nose

up in the air. "But they said that my whale statue alone raised enough money to meet their goal for the whole year!"

"Wait," Dad said. "Tell them the best part."

"Oh, right," Mom said, still lighting up the room with her smile. "When everyone had calmed down, the woman who bid so high—Mrs. Montgomery—came up to me, introduced herself, and asked if I could make her a smaller version that she could have for her home. Of course I said yes, and she actually hugged me! Then she told someone else, who told someone else, who told someone else. And suddenly I have eight appointments tomorrow at the store to sell miniature whale sculptures!"

"It's like what Mitch always says: 'Word of mouth is really powerful'! Right?" Dad added.

"Well, I may have said something like that once or twice," I said. "Oh, and when you make the little whales, guys, don't make too many."

"We know," Dad said proudly. "We already talked about that. If we make so many that they're not rare, the price will go down."

"Supply and demand," Mom added.

The next morning, I wasn't sure if I'd just fallen asleep again after that—or if I'd totally passed out.

———

For weeks I had been looking forward to the season-ending football game between Jonasburg and Clarksville. It was a day away, which meant this would be the last football practice of the season. Which meant this would be my last day cleaning up the locker rooms.

Honestly, it never really felt like that much of a punishment (as long as I could stay away from Clint Grayson). I mean, if I never had to pick up a Gatorade bottle again, that would be fine with me. But I kind of liked feeling like I was a part of the team—even if I never put on a uniform or a helmet. I liked talking with Coach Williams. And I liked talking with Mr. Eads, too.

On this day, Mr. Eads was already folding uniforms when I arrived. And he was wearing a Jonasburg football sweatshirt that said EADS on the back, with a number 55.

"Cool jersey!" I said.

"Yeah, I wear it every year before the Clarksville game. Not sure if it's good luck or bad luck, but I figure at least the kids know I'm supporting them."

"Why did you choose number fifty-five?" I asked.

"I didn't," he said. "Coach Williams gave it to me a few years back when I turned fifty-five. I don't even know how he found out it was my birthday. That's the kind of guy he is."

The thought hung in the air. Then Mr. Eads shook his head. "Be a shame to lose a guy like that."

"You heard, too, huh?" I said.

"Whole town is talking about it—" Mr. Eads stopped abruptly and looked over my shoulder. "Speak of the devil!"

I turned around, and there was Coach Williams. He looked like a man who hadn't slept since summer vacation. His face was covered with the beginning of a beard and looked like a field that needed mowing. His hair spiked out in different directions. The bags around his eyes looked like doughnuts.

Still, he was cheerful, the way a real leader is supposed to be. "Hey, guys! Great work on the uniforms all season. We may not win every game—well, far from it—but thanks to you, Eads, we always look better than the other guys!"

Mr. Eads just nodded, but I could tell that Coach Williams had made his day. "Mitch," the coach went on. "Come see me one second, if you could."

I followed him into his office. It reminded me of walking into the office of Assistant Principal Allegra. On the wall there was a picture of Coach Williams from when he played football at Indiana University. He looked a lot happier then. There was also a picture of his family, his wife and their two kids, who looked to be about eight and six. It made me sad to think that if Jonasburg lost to Clarksville, their dad was going to get fired and they would probably have to move to a different school. Sort of like I had.

"You got any football advice for an old man?" he asked.

I sure did.

I asked Coach Williams if he remembered this situation from the game against Bloomington High School North: Jonasburg had the ball past midfield, near the 35-yard line. It was fourth down and three yards to go. It was out of reach for the Jonasburg kicker to attempt a field goal, so Coach Williams decided to punt. The punt landed in the end zone, a touchback, and Bloomington North started with the ball back at their own twenty-yard line.

"Yes, I remember," he said. "Why do you bring it up?"

"Well, why did you decide to punt?" I asked.

"I dunno," he said, shrugging. "I guess that's what my gut said to do."

"But *why* did your gut say to punt?"

"Because it was fourth down," he said flatly. "That's what you do, last time I checked."

Check again, I thought to myself.

"You decided not to kick a field goal, which was smart. And you decided not to go for it on fourth down and you punted instead. The Cougars got the ball back on the twenty-yard line."

"Right..."

"So look at it this way. If you go for it on fourth-and-three, the chances of making it are around fifty percent. A coin flip. So you either succeed, stay on offense, and maybe score a touchdown. Or you fail. But what happens when you fail? The other team gets the ball at the thirty-five-yard line. Only fifteen yards better off than they would be if you had punted. Does that make sense?"

"Sort of," he said.

"For fifteen lousy yards, wouldn't you take a fifty-fifty chance that you'll keep the ball and let your offense stay on the field?"

"Well, yeah," Coach Williams said. "If you had explained it to me that way at the time, I definitely would have gone for it on fourth down."

"And that would have been the right move," I added, to make sure he got the point.

Coach Williams looked out, like he was staring at a point on the horizon only he could see. I could tell that he was deep in thought.

"But let me ask you this, then," he said. "In *most* cases, wouldn't you be better off going for it on fourth down and not punting? I mean, if you want to hang on to the ball as much as possible, and you're successful going for it on fourth half the time, and even when you fail you're not giving up that many yards, shouldn't you avoid punting just about every time?"

"Just about," I responded.

"Interesting. Very interesting," he said. "Must make sense sometimes to not attempt a field goal either, right?"

"Yep," I agreed. "You're often better off keeping the ball and going for a touchdown than attempting the field goal. I know the three points are tempting, but if you keep the ball longer you might score a touchdown and you can always kick a field goal later if the drive stalls then."

Coach Williams whistled. "I know one kid who won't be happy to hear that idea."

"Who's that?" I asked.

"Clint Grayson. You know him?"

"You could say that."

"Well, he and his dad are already talking about how he's going to be the star kicker when he comes in next year as a freshman. Probably be the first freshman to start for the team in a decade. If he expects to be a star, and we don't punt or kick field goals much, that could be a problem. Maybe he'll need to learn to play another position."

I tried my hardest to hold back a smile. I had

just gotten revenge on the biggest bully in school, and I hadn't even planned it that way. I couldn't wait to tell Jamie!

Then Mr. Williams brought me back down to earth. "Of course, if I get fired after this season, who knows what'll happen? For all we know, a new coach might come in who will want to kick on *third* down."

"Or maybe we'll win tomorrow and it won't come to that," I said hopefully. Then it occurred to me that maybe it sounded weird to say *we'll win*, since I wasn't part of the team. "Or *you'll* win."

"No, you were right the first time. *We'll* win. You're part of this team now."

When we lived in California, every year they held a foot race from the San Francisco Bay to the Pacific Ocean. Most of the runners would go dressed in crazy costumes—circus clowns and avocados and bank robbers and Marilyn Monroes. Lots of Marilyn Monroes. If you lived somewhere else, you would probably think it was weird. But if you were from San Francisco, the race was a tradition and it seemed perfectly normal.

Same thing with the Jonasburg-Clarksville football game. If you weren't living in the area, you might think it was weird that so many people would get so worked up over a bunch of teenagers playing a high school football game. But it seemed normal to us. It was our Super Bowl.

Everyone from both towns dressed in the colors of the school they supported. Before the game, the only traffic jam of the year happened as cars lined State Route 11, leading to the football stadium. The newspaper had a special section called "The Game." The local radio station, WRUB, had a pre-game show that started three hours before.

Mom, Dad, and I listened to the show in the car while we were stuck in traffic. During an interview with Coach Williams, the host said, "How are you handling the pressure of a make-or-break game like this?"

"We treat it like any other game," Coach said, sounding calm.

"Any tricks up your sleeve?" the man asked.

Coach Williams chuckled. "We may have a few secret weapons on the sidelines tonight."

I did a little fist pump in the backseat when I heard that.

Finally, the traffic moved, and I quickly left Mom and Dad to meet Jamie in front of the concession stand. Each of us brought a clipboard containing the "nuggets" we had discovered. Wearing "Full Access" badges around our necks, we walked right onto the field.

It was like everyone was making preparations before showtime. The band was warming up. The cheerleaders were practicing their routines. The officials were stretching their legs. We were on the sidelines near midfield when a familiar voice sliced through the air.

"Hey, Mitchy. You and your girlfriend can't be on the field. It's only for players. And if we know anything, it's that you're not a player."

It was Clint Grayson, the human rash. And he was coming right at me.

CHAPTER 17

SECRET WEAPON

Before Jamie could say something—probably about his awful breath—I just smiled and pointed to our badges.

He stopped in his tracks, shocked. "It'll be different next year," he managed to get out, "when I'm on the varsity team and you'll be up in the bleachers cheering for me."

"That's what you think," Jamie muttered under her breath.

We smiled at each other.

At 6:30, the team ran onto the field. The cheerleaders held up some giant paper wall in the shape of a J. Kevin broke through and the rest of the team followed. On the Jonasburg side, the crowd went bananas, while the Clarksville side booed. When Clarksville ran out, it was the other way around.

I watched as Coach Williams walked onto the field. He took an extra long look at the bleachers and the band and the whole crazy scene. Then he took a deep breath. When he saw us, he jogged right over. "My secret weapons!" he exclaimed, bumping our fists. "Don't leave my side!"

Two players from each team trotted to the middle of the field for the coin flip. Jonasburg won, and chose to receive the kickoff. Coach Williams turned to us. "Any last-minute advice?"

"Let Kevin return the kick," Jamie said, remembering our discovery: When Kevin had the ball in his hands, Jonasburg gained almost three times as many yards as they did otherwise.

Without even looking over at us, Coach Williams yelled out to the team, "Let Sloan field it!" Sure enough, the ball spun through the air and came to Kevin, who was standing at the twenty-yard line. As soon as he cradled it, he started running. He wasn't tackled until he was at midfield, which meant he'd run it back thirty yards—almost the exact average we had calculated.

I was happy Jamie had made the right call. And I was happy that the system was working already. But I also felt a tiny bit jealous. Especially when she gave me a smug look that said *Top that, pal!*

So I tried to. I slid right next to Coach Williams. "Throw a pass on first down," I said, remembering how Neil was most successful when he threw the ball right away. Nodding, Coach Williams called for a passing play. Neil took the ball, scooted a few steps to his right, and threw it to Nathan Isaac.

Ever since his embarrassment earlier in the season, people had been calling Nathan "the Wrong Way Kid," and his YouTube views had grown to over 2.5 million at this point—but this time he made sure he was headed in the right direction, gaining nine yards. On the Jonasburg side of the stands, the fans shrieked and cheered. On the sidelines, I shot Jamie a look. *Not bad, huh? Your turn.*

As the teams went back and forth, Jamie and I had our own little game, trying to come up with the better idea to give Coach Williams. At the end of the first quarter, neither team had scored. But then Jonasburg struck at the beginning of the second quarter. Throwing the ball again on first down, Neil took a few steps back, looking for a receiver. Just as the Clarksville tacklers were getting ready to grab him, he flung the ball downfield as far as he could.

Three Clarksville players were waiting in the end zone, ready to make the interception. But, fortunately, Kevin was there, too. As if climbing some invisible ladder, he jumped up higher than the players on the other team. At the height of his leap, he caught the ball and held on to it when he landed. Touchdown!

The band started playing; the cheerleaders started jumping. I turned to the Jonasburg section of the crowd, just in time to see my parents kiss. Ick. On the field, players smacked Kevin on the back of his helmet. He calmly flipped the ball to the official, like he hadn't done anything special.

I could hear his voice in my head. *When you score a touchdown, act like you've been there before, Mitch.*

When the halftime horn sounded, Jonasburg was leading 7–0. As the team trotted off to the locker room, Jamie and I walked to the concession stand. Of course, Ben Barnes was already there, picking up his order of nachos with a corn dog lying on top in the middle. "Hey, guys," he said. "Have a bite, and I promise you won't make that face."

"No, really, it's okay," Jamie said. "Some of us want to live to be adults."

Just then a woman poked Jamie on the shoulder.

"Oh, hey, Mom," she said.

I almost didn't recognize Mrs. Spielberger. She wasn't wearing her usual fancy clothes and sunglasses that even I could tell were expensive. Instead, she was dressed up in maroon and gold and even had a whale painted on the side of her face.

"Hey, guys!" she said. "I don't know what you're doing, but it seems to be working. Dad is explaining football to me and I think I'm starting to get it!"

Right about then, I saw my parents.

"Your dad and I are so proud," Mom said. "We're sitting up there and can't believe that both our kids are on the field at the same time!"

"And you're both following your bliss," Dad said.

I wasn't sure what he meant, but his hippie talk was starting to grow on me a little. It might actually be kind of cool that he used words that no other parents used.

"I'm glad we found you right now, Mitch," said Dad. "They're about to make our announcement."

Before I could ask what he meant, the band finished up the halftime performance, the baton girl caught the stick she had thrown a mile in the air, and then the announcer's voice boomed: "Another round of applause for the Whales marching band. And a reminder, this halftime show was brought to you by Sloans' Creations on Seventh Street, Jonasburg's oldest art studio. That's Sloans' Creations, for the grooviest paintings, sculptures, and fine art in Indiana."

Dad had wrapped his arm around Mom's shoulders. "You always told us to advertise," he said. "We had some extra money after all the sales we made in the last few days. So we figured why not do it at the biggest football game of the year?"

I didn't know what to say. So I quickly looked around to make sure no one was watching, then I hugged Mom and Dad.

"Let's go, Mitch!" Jamie called. She was already halfway back to the sidelines.

Before the second half started, Coach Williams met up with Jamie and me, asking if we had any last-minute advice. Again, she was right on top of it. "You might want to give the officials a friendly reminder that Clarksville hasn't been called for pass interference *once* this entire season!"

I could tell he liked that one. With Jamie and me trailing behind like a rudder on a boat, Coach Williams found two officials and put his arms around their shoulders. "Great game so far, gentlemen," he said cheerily. "Just a gentle reminder: Watch for the pass interference when we throw the ball. Crazy as this sounds, Clarksville hasn't been called for that penalty once all year. Can you believe it?"

The officials didn't answer. In fact, their faces were as still as statues. They just kept staring straight ahead. But, in the nicest way possible, Coach Williams had planted a little seed in their brains. He'd just gently suggested that maybe, just maybe, the refs at all of Clarksville's other games hadn't really been doing their jobs.

So now *these* refs would want to look better. If pass interference was going on, they'd be the ones to catch it.

The third quarter played out a lot like the first two. Clarksville would march the ball downfield, but the Jonasburg defense would eventually stop them. Then Jonasburg would head the other way, but the Clarksville defense would prevent any scoring.

With a few minutes left in the quarter, Jonasburg had the ball near midfield. It was third down, and Neil threw a pass to Kevin. The defender and Kevin both jumped for it, and it looked to me like the defender hit Kevin's hands before the ball did. But the whistle didn't blow, so it was just an incomplete pass. With fourth down coming up, Coach Williams looked over at me. "I'm taking your advice, Sloan," he said. "We're going to go for it. We're not going to punt." He took a deep breath and added, "If we're going down, we're going down swinging!"

But it turned out that Coach Williams didn't even have to make the choice. It came a few seconds later than normal, but a yellow penalty flag flew through the air and landed softly on the ground. The ref signaled pass interference on Clarksville. The fifteen-yard penalty made it first down, Jonasburg.

Who knows? Maybe the refs would have seen that pass interference even if Coach Williams had said nothing. But Jamie and I like to think we had something to do with that penalty. The power of suggestion.

Even after they got the benefit of the very first pass interference call made against Clarksville all season, Jonasburg failed to score. And then Clarksville failed to score. Then Jonasburg. Then Clarksville. In the week heading up to the game, I heard a radio announcer predict that it would be "a high-scoring affair." I kept wondering how he felt about that prediction as I looked at the scoreboard and saw the numbers frozen—Home 7, Away 0. All the while, the time on the clock kept dwindling down.

And then it happened. A play that made me feel sick to my stomach. With barely four minutes to go in the game, Jonasburg had the ball at the ten-yard line. The Whales were ninety yards away from scoring another touchdown, but if they played it right, they could run out the clock.

On first down, Neil passed again. This time, he tossed a quick pass to Kevin, who caught the ball cleanly. He danced away from a Clarksville player but then headed backward—never a good idea—and slipped on a wet patch of grass. As he tried to catch his balance, the ball squirted right out of his hands.

Kevin lunged, but a Clarksville player beat him to it, pouncing on the ball like a cat on a mouse. Suddenly, Clarksville had the ball at the one-yard line, thirty-six inches away from tying the game. Or maybe even winning.

The Clarksville crowd shrieked. The Jonasburg crowd groaned. Coach Williams looked like he had just seen a ghost. Kevin lay on the field, both hands on his helmet.

This was awful to watch. It wasn't fair, but

I knew how sports worked: If Jonasburg lost the game, he would be blamed for it.

Out of the corner of my eye, I caught the expression on Jamie's face. "It'll be okay, Mitch," she said, sounding more like she was trying to convince herself than like she actually believed it.

As usual, Coach Williams was upbeat. "It's okay," he said, clapping his hands together. "We're just gonna have to stop 'em."

And Jonasburg did on the first play, tackling a Clarksville running back almost as soon as he got the ball. And they did on the second play, too, when A.J. Kumar tackled the Clarksville quarterback right at the line of scrimmage. On third down, Jonasburg stopped Clarksville again, this time batting away a pass.

Just like that, it was fourth down. One yard to go. Three minutes left in the game. Jonasburg 7, Clarksville 0. Fans on both sides of the field were going positively nuts.

Clarksville called a time-out. They had a big choice to make. Would they go for it or kick a field goal? The field goal was almost a sure thing. But if they made it, the score would be 7–3 and they would have to score again. And since their defense had been solid all second half—Jonasburg hadn't scored a point since the touchdown—they were likely to get the ball back. Going for a touchdown, on the other hand, would be riskier. But it would have more reward, too. If they scored, they'd probably tie the game.

After the time-out, the Clarksville players ran onto the field, including their kicker, who began practicing, whipping his foot through the air.

Something didn't feel right to me. Without even thinking about it, I tapped Coach Williams's elbow. "Call time-out," I said.

"Huh?"

"Call time-out," I said. "It's a fake."

He made a T with his hands, and the referees called time-out. Coach Williams turned to me and walked us a few feet away from everyone else.

"What's this about, Mitch?"

"They're going to fake the field goal."

"How do you know?"

That was a good question. And I didn't have time

to explain it. But when Jamie and I were running the gambling pool, we noticed that our customers hated losing ten dollars a lot more than they liked winning eight dollars. When they won, they were happy, but it was like they had expected it. When they lost, it really stung.

And they would do anything to prevent feeling that way.

Clarksville had probably come into this game expecting to win. Looking at our record all season, they had every reason to think they'd beat us, just like so many other teams had. And now they had the ball on the one-yard line. In their minds, that was practically a touchdown.

But they hadn't gotten it yet. They'd gained zero yards in their last three plays, and they were looking at losing the six points they'd thought they'd already won. They would do anything not to let that happen.

The Clarksville players seemed to indicate a fake field goal, too. They were pretty hyper, even anxious. Like they couldn't wait to hike the ball. Also, I noticed that they had three players on the field who they normally didn't use for kicks. Because I had watched all that film with Jamie on Clarksville's games, I now noticed that numbers 50, 77, and 66 were replaced by numbers 12, 34, and 80. That said to me that something different was going on.

They weren't going to settle for three points. They weren't going to try for a field goal.

"Just trust me," I said firmly.

"Okay, guys!" Coach Williams said, walking back to the team. "Prepare for the fake field goal. My secret weapon thinks they're going for the touchdown."

The teams charged back onto the field. Clarksville again lined up for the field goal. The ref blew the whistle to start play. When the Clarksville center snapped the ball to the holder, he immediately stood up and began to run. A fake! Just as I suspected!

And just as every Jonasburg player expected. They chased the runner down before he'd gone five steps. It was hard to say who actually tackled him, because any of a dozen arms grabbed the poor kid and pushed him back several yards to the ground. He didn't come close to scoring.

Coach Williams looked at me and winked. The Jonasburg players on the sidelines and their fans in the stands went crazy.

Secret weapon? I kind of liked that.

Jonasburg got the ball back. Now, if this were one of those sports movies, we would go on to score the winning touchdown in the last second. But that didn't exactly happen.

It didn't need to.

Without turning to us for advice, Coach Williams looked calm as could be and addressed the team on the sidelines. "We want to run out the clock, guys," he said. "Three things stop the clock. Who knows what they are?"

Even in the last moments of the Big Game, Coach Williams was teaching. *No wonder all the players like him*, I thought to myself.

Neil spoke first. "Running out of bounds, throwing an incomplete pass, and getting called for a penalty."

"Right! So no running out of bounds. No passing. No penalties. And no fumbling, Kevin Sloan," Coach

Williams said, smiling and winking. Kevin smiled back, relieved that his disaster hadn't turned out to be so disastrous. "And we win this game!"

And they did.

Jonasburg ran three plays, got a first down, and then ran out the clock as time expired. The scoreboard froze.

Jonasburg 7, Clarksville 0.

The noise from the final horn was still hanging in the air when the Jonasburg fans stormed onto the field, jumping and dancing and shouting. A group of players ran over to Kevin. A few minutes earlier, he had almost cost his team the game. Now he was the hero, the only player to score. That's sports.

Suspended on his teammates' shoulders, holding his helmet in his hand, sweat making his eye black streak down his cheeks, he looked into the crowd. When our eyes met, he just nodded. I nodded back. We practically had a whole conversation right there, without using a single word.

I looked for Coach Williams, but he had thrown his ball cap up in the air and then sprinted to the fence, where his wife and children were waiting for him. I guess they weren't going to have to change schools after all.

Later, Coach Williams told me that Principal Pearlman had called him at home that night and said, "Let's build on this next season." It was his way of saying, *You still have your job.*

As for Jamie and me, as soon as the game ended, we jumped into each other's arms. Everyone else was hugging, so why shouldn't we? Then we realized what we were doing and let go at the same time. Awkward. We bumped fists instead.

"We did it!" she said. "How do you feel?"

"Better than I ever did making lots of money," I replied. "That's for sure."

We walked off the field and were barely at the gate when we heard our names. It was Mr. Rafferty, whose smile was as big as a cantaloupe slice. He was standing with his wife. "Did you see these two on the field tonight?" he asked her. "Coach Williams told me that they're his two star *math*letes." His wife rolled her eyes, but she was smiling, and Jamie and I were too happy to groan at his pun this time.

While his wife was chatting with Jamie, Mr. R. turned to me, "You know," he said, "I was really disappointed in you earlier this year. I had hoped you would see what you were doing was wrong and stop your little operation on your own. But when that notebook was discovered, I had to tell Assistant Principal Allegra what I'd seen."

"I know," I said. "You'd tried to warn me. I didn't want to listen."

"I believe in second chances, Mitch," he continued. "You now have a second chance at this school. Use it wisely." There were no puns, no jokes, and no usual goofiness in his voice. "Just remember, *friends* aren't forged out of supply and demand, right?"

Translation: *Mitch, if people are nice just because you do things for them, then they're not really your friends.*

I nodded and thanked Mr. R., who once again reminded me why he was my favorite teacher.

As he and his wife walked off, Jamie and I started walking to meet up with our parents. But we were stopped again, this time by a tall, slender man wearing a hoodie. The words "Jonasburg Regional Hoops" were stitched on the front.

"Hey, it's Mitch and Jamie, right?"

"Right," we said.

"I'm Coach Wahl!" he said excitedly. "Let me ask you guys something: What do you know about basketball?"

Michael Lebrecht

L. Jon Wertheim is an executive editor for *Sports Illustrated*, a regular contributor to CNN and NPR, and the author of several books, including *Scorecasting: The Hidden Influences Behind How Sports are Played and Games are Won*, which he coauthored with Tobias Moskowitz. He lives with his wife and two kids in New York City.

Beth Rooney

Tobias Moskowitz is a financial economist and the Fama Family Professor of Finance at the University of Chicago Booth School of Business. He was the winner of the 2007 American Finance Association Fischer Black Prize, biennially awarded to the leading financial scholar in the world under the age of forty. He lives with his wife and four kids in Chicago.

Jon and Toby are childhood friends from Indiana. Toby is an economist interested in sports, and Jon is a sports-media figure interested in finance, which led to their collaboration on their bestselling book, *Scorecasting*. They were then inspired to write a children's book that explores similar topics as those in their adult book, combining sports, statistics, and financial literacy in a fun story for kids.